A DEADLY DISTANCE

THE JACK NOBLE SERIES™ BOOK TWO

L.T. RYAN

LIQUID MIND MEDIA, LLC

For information contact:

ltryan70@gmail.com

http://LTRyan.com

https://www.facebook.com/JackNobleBooks

This book is dedicated to Gabriella. Thank you for your patience, support, belief and inspiration. And for putting up with my incessant talk about Jack Noble and his cast of derelict friends and foes. Without you, this book would have never taken shape.

I also thank you, the reader, for taking a chance on an unknown author and a character named Jack Noble. I hope he becomes as much a part of your life as he is mine.

THE JACK NOBLE SERIES

Receive a free copy of The Recruit by visiting http://ltryan.com/newsletter.

1

December 19, 2004

Six feet. A deadly distance. Especially when one man has a gun aimed at another. Close enough to take missing out of the equation. Far enough away that the target has slightly more than a zero percent chance of making a move, whether to disarm the assailant or duck and cover.

The guy I'd been hunting in the dusty and dimly lit warehouse found me first. I had taken a set of splintered wooden stairs to the catwalk that wrapped the interior edges of the building and cut across the center of the large rectangular room. I hustled up the steps, two at a time. The old wooden boards sagged and creaked and moaned, but held under my weight. The catwalk was stronger, sturdier. It didn't move in response to me. No bouncing. No side-to-side sway. One foot fell in front of the other as I sidestepped along the catwalk. I let my feet hit the floor from the outside in, minimizing the noise. Still, the planks gave off a slight thump in response to my boots hitting the wood. I knew if I wasn't careful, he'd hear me.

And he did.

Fortunately, I heard his footsteps, too. Unfortunately, I only heard them a second before he spoke.

"Stop," he said. His accent was thick, perhaps South American. "Drop your gun."

I froze and lifted my hands, letting the gun swing like a pendulum, upside down and with only my index finger holding it up by the trigger guard.

"Drop it," he said.

I dipped my finger to the side and let the gun slide off and over the railing. It hit the floor with a thud, managing to keep from discharging a round. The cold handle of my backup piece rested reassuringly against my lower back, sending chills through me as the cold metal touched my sweaty skin.

"Now turn around," he said.

I turned in a half-circle and got my first good look at the man I'd been chasing for the last twenty minutes. He stood approximately five foot nine and weighed probably one-eighty. He wore a tan jacket and black knit cap. Sparse dark hair covered his cheeks and chin. His eyes matched his hair. He stood six feet away, a pistol held close to his chest and aimed at me.

A distance of six feet increased his odds of being deadly accurate.

A distance of six feet reduced my chances of effectively neutralizing him.

Even at six-two, my reach wasn't enough to land an effective blow in this situation.

"Who the hell are you?" he said.

"I'm the man who was sent to kill you," I said.

"By who?"

"What?"

"Who's your boss?"

"Why?"

"Because I want to write him a letter to recommend he fires you."

I chuckled. The guy had a sense of humor, only the look on his face said he wasn't joking.

"Why's that?" I said.

"Because you failed this class, asshole." He lifted the barrel of the gun and waved it back and forth, like a mother scolding her toddler.

"Only problem," I said, "is this is only recess. Playtime for you."

The man forced a laugh. "You're the one following me, so you must have some idea who I am."

"Not really." And that was the truth. Frank Skinner and I had acted on a single piece of information that said a man fitting the guy's description would be waiting at a bus stop.

"Well, let me give you the abridged version," he said. "I'm someone you shouldn't be following. You should have done your homework first. Now it's too late for you."

I smiled. "First, enough with the school analogies. Second, it's never too late for me."

His eyes narrowed. He brought his left hand up and wiped his cheek with his palm. His eyes darted upward and mine followed along. Light shone through a tiny hole in the roof. Bright, but gray. Rainwater dripped through the hole and spattered the man's face. He cursed under his breath as a bead of water slapped against his cheek. He'd have to move and his next step would seal my fate.

The man didn't move, though. Not immediately, at least. Two more drops hit him, then a third. Finally, he cursed and took a step forward. Six feet had been reduced to five. Still out of my reach, but not by much. If I lunged forward, I could reach him in one step instead of two.

"Give it up," I said. "We've got the warehouse surrounded. You won't make it out of here."

"Then neither will you." His eyes widened and he stuck his arm all the way out. Another mistake. His wrist flicked up and down, jerking the gun in and out of aim.

I saw my opportunity. The distance between the gun and me had been reduced by at least two-and-a-half feet. A full step and I'd have him by the wrist, neutralizing the immediate threat.

A crashing sound to my right startled both of us. I turned my head and saw a door to the outside open. Light flooded the ground floor of the warehouse and the silhouette of a man slipped through the opening and then disappeared into the shadows. I had lied when I said we had the building surrounded. There were only two of us, and I had left Frank behind a block away from the building. Either he had caught up, or the man hadn't been alone, in which case it would be two against me.

"Freeze!" Frank's voice echoed through the warehouse.

The man forgot about me and turned toward Frank. Bright muzzle blast exploded in front of me as the man opened fire on my partner.

Frank didn't return fire, hopefully in an effort to avoid wounding me, and not because he'd been hit. I couldn't worry about that, though. The man stood five feet away, his body turned and his arms outstretched over the steel railing. The time to make a move was now.

I lunged forward, left arm out, right arm up, closing the distance before the man could react. I wrapped my left hand around his throat from the side, letting my thumb slide below his Adam's apple. He grunted against the pressure. At the same time I drove my right arm down, catching him on his wrist, which extended out a few feet over the railing. I twisted his arm and drove it down into the steel railing. Bone and steel met with a sickening crack followed by the sounds of the man screaming. His broken arm and spasming muscles could no longer muster up the strength required to hold the sidearm, and he dropped it. It hit the floor below us with a clank.

"Frank?" I yelled.

No answer.

The man reached across his body with his left arm and punched at my face, his fist connecting with my nose. Although he didn't have enough momentum to do any real damage, the blow managed to disrupt my grip on his neck. The center of my face stung and my eyes flooded with tears. I felt him break away from my grasp.

"My arm," he said. "You bastard, you broke my damn arm."

I heard the sound of a knife being pulled from a sheath, blade against leather. I brought my palms to my eyes and wiped away the tears that blurred my vision. Once again, the man stood six feet away from me. His fractured right arm pressed against his chest. In his left, he held a knife with a six-inch blade. The light caught and winked off the stainless steel as he twirled it in his palm.

This time six feet didn't matter. I didn't have to contend with a bullet. In a fluid motion, I lunged forward and grabbed the railing on either side with both hands. Then I swung my legs forward while drawing my knees in. I drove the soles of my combat boots into his chest. He shrieked as they connected with his broken arm. The knife fell from his hand and bounced off the catwalk and fell to the concrete warehouse floor.

My momentum carried my body through, knocking the man down. He turned onto his stomach and began crawling away. His left arm scraped and scratched against the worn wooden planks while his right dragged behind, bent awkwardly at the wrist.

"Jack," Frank shouted from below.

I walked up behind the man and stood over him and said nothing. I reached down and wrapped my right arm around his neck. His pulse thumped hard against the crook of my arm. I reached around with my left arm and grabbed my right elbow and pulled back hard. The movement squeezed the man's neck shut. I didn't care whether he died from asphyxiation, a broken neck, or if his head popped off.

The man clawed at my forearm. He swung his hips side to side, but he was no match for me. Desperate attempts to breathe were cut off by the force I exerted against his trachea.

"Jack, let him go."

I looked up and saw Frank standing at the end of the catwalk.

"Come on, Jack," he said. "We need this guy. He's got info for us."

"I don't care," I said as I squeezed tighter.

Frank approached with a hint of caution, perhaps thinking I'd snapped. He'd have been right if he thought it, too. "Let him go, Jack. Let's get him to the office and question him. Then you can do whatever you want to him."

The man's knit cap had fallen off and his sweat soaked hair brushed against my face as his body went limp. I pulled back and looked at Frank and then the man. Frank's words filtered through the rage that kept me from thinking straight, and suddenly they made sense. I let go of the man and his body fell against the catwalk, limp and lifeless.

I reached over and grabbed the railing and pulled myself up. "Christ, I think I killed him."

Frank tucked his gun and squatted down. He reached out and placed his hand on the man's neck. After a few seconds, he said, "He's got a pulse. Help me get him downstairs and into the car."

"So that's where you were," I said. "Pulling the car around instead of chasing him in here with me."

"You took off, Jack. I lost you." He looked up and I met his gaze with a smile.

"Only giving you a hard time." I bent over, scooped my hands under the man's shoulders, and lifted him up. Frank grabbed his legs and we carried him down the rickety stairs, which screamed in response to close to six hundred pounds of force pressing down on them.

Frank had parked the car right outside the warehouse entrance, trunk to door.

"I'm going to make sure it's clear out there," he said.

I nodded and leaned against the heavy steel framed door for support. The man started to come to. He coughed a few times and a deep, guttural groan emanated from his throat. I thought about rendering him unconscious again, but decided against it. A blow to the head might dampen his memory, and we needed to know everything he knew.

Frank opened the back door on the driver's side of his Lincoln and gestured for me to come out.

I backed out of the warehouse, dragging the guy with me. I looked to the left and to the right. The area was empty. I didn't bother to stare into windows, though. If someone was watching us, so be it. We'd be gone by the time the cops came. And even if they caught up to us, there was little they could do. We were, for all intents and purposes, untouchable.

The rain had stopped and the sun peeked through the melting clouds. The light penetrated my eyes like shards of glass. Cold wind whipped around the sides of the building, meeting at the spot where I stood. It felt like being pelted with icy snowballs from both sides.

"Give me a hand," I said.

Frank came closer and reached out for the man's right arm in an effort to stabilize it. Together we slid him into the back seat and buckled him in. I handcuffed his left wrist to the metal post that connected the headrest to the front passenger's seat.

"Sit in back with him," Frank said. "If he gets out of line," he looked at the man and smiled, "well, you know what to do."

I nodded, then walked around the back of the car and got in on the opposite side. I slid in next to the man and, for the first time, realized that he smelled like he hadn't showered in a week.

"If you hadn't been armed, I'd have thought you were a bum," I said.

The man pursed his lips and spit, his saliva smattering the back of the seat in front of him as well as the center console next to Frank.

I drove my elbow into his solar plexus. He coughed an exhale as the air drained from his lungs. His body doubled over, chin to knees.

"Try it again," I said.

He turned his head toward me. His face was deep red and the veins in his forehead stuck out like a snake swimming through water. His mouth opened and closed like a fish out of water as he tried to suck in air, but couldn't.

"Keep him quiet," Frank said.

I nodded while staring at the man as he held his arm close to his chest. I said to Frank, "Go ahead and call the doc in to set and splint that arm."

2

Frank drove us to SIS's unofficial headquarters. Though we said unofficial, the building outside of Washington, D.C. was our primary location. However, any building we occupied for the purpose of advancing our mission would be considered our headquarters and always labeled unofficial. The SIS was an agency that didn't exist. The primary focus of the group was counter-terrorism. We had complete and total autonomy. We could push any other agency to the back of the line if we felt our cause took precedence. The agents in our group were considered elite, and often handpicked from among the top recruits of the CIA, FBI and DEA. Only a handful of politicians and higher ups in the military knew of the agency's existence, and if you asked them, they'd flat out deny it, even if there was a gun to their head.

We pulled up around the rear of the building. Frank stopped in front of what appeared to be a wall. If you stood close enough, and in the right spot, you'd see a tiny crack that ran up its center, then turned to the right and met another thin crack. Frank pulled a device out of his pocket and pushed a button. A wide door opened out and Frank drove into a dark garage. The place was empty except for my car, a large SUV, and a four-door maroon Lexus that belonged to the doctor.

I waited in the back seat after Frank parked and cut the engine. He got out, walked around the back and opened the door next to the man. I removed the handcuff from his left wrist and pushed the man out while Frank pulled. The guy stumbled out and fell to the ground. He groaned and clutched at his broken arm.

"Get up," Frank told the guy.

I slid through the open door. The guy was on his knees, bent over with his forehead resting on the concrete floor. I grabbed him by his shirt collar and pulled the man's upper body straight up. Frank reached under his left arm and started pulling. I grabbed his collar and the waistband of his pants. We got him to his feet, and then led him to the only door in the garage.

Frank swiped an access card through a security card reader and the light changed from red to green. He then placed his thumb on a pad. There was a series of beeps, and another light turned from red to green. Then the lock clicked and Frank turned the door handle. We walked down a short hall and came to the area of the main floor that we called the lobby. There were two doors on the far wall. Each door led to an interrogation room. A four by six foot mirrored window was placed a foot away from each door. Opposite the interrogation rooms was our infirmary, a state of the art medical facility that was equipped for everything from bee stings to surgery. There were six offices in the lobby, three on the north wall, and three on the south. My office was next to Frank's. The third office on our side was designated for all of team B.

The stale air of the lobby enveloped us. The smell of ammonia hardly affected me anymore, but the guy we were dragging down the hall coughed and gagged as he breathed in the fumes.

The doctor stood in the doorway of the infirmary. He was tall and middle aged. His full head of hair was half brown, half gray. His long, pointy nose was the only distinguishing feature on his face. He nodded toward our prisoner. "What's wrong with him?"

"Broken arm," I said. "Maybe a concussion, too. But that shouldn't matter."

The doctor shrugged and nodded over his shoulder. "Drop him in there."

"You want one of us to stay?" I asked.

"Him." The doctor pointed at Frank. "You ask too many questions, Mr. Noble."

Frank laughed and the doctor joined in. I said nothing. He had a point. I did tend to ask a lot of questions when he was working on one of us. I often thought that if my life had gone a bit differently when I was young, I could have ended up a doctor or trauma surgeon.

I left the infirmary and went to my office. I stacked a few manila folders and moved them to the corner of the desk, then started a pot of coffee. The rich aroma of the dark grinds soaked the air in my office. I didn't feel like waiting for the full pot to brew, so I emptied it into a stained mug as soon as there was enough. I held the mug in both hands and leaned back in my chair. The caffeine coursed through my veins, providing the jolt I needed.

I got up and left my office and walked back to the infirmary. Frank glanced at me and said nothing. He concentrated on the guy's broken arm. I took a few more steps and stopped inside the doorway and leaned against the frame.

"Out," the doctor said.

I could tell by his tone that he was serious. We tried hard to avoid pissing Doc off, because you never knew when you were going to need him to treat you. I shrugged and backed up a few feet. Turned around and leaned back against the wall a couple yards from the door. I lifted the coffee to my face and inhaled. Steam singed the inside of my nose for a second. I took a sip. It was strong. Perhaps a bit too strong, if there was such a thing. I decided it didn't matter. The brew helped clear the cobwebs from my head, and that was always welcome.

Behind me, I heard the sound of bone grating against bone. The doctor was setting the fracture. The man screamed as his ulna and then radius were placed in their natural positions. I took his cries of pain as a sign that the doctor hadn't bothered to numb the guy up. I was OK with that, and apparently Frank was too. Why waste our supplies on a criminal?

With the doctor almost finished, I started to think about what questions to ask the man. We didn't know much about him, except that he showed up at a place that our intel indicated would be a spot where something would happen. But we had no idea who this guy was. What was he doing near the bus stop? Was he a part of the group we were tracking, or doing business with them? Why did he run from us? Why did he try to kill me?

Both Frank and I had a feeling we were closing in on some-thing big. Every piece of evidence we had gathered so far pointed to this being a terrorist cell. The only good thing about that was that we didn't have to turn it over to the FBI or DEA. These guys had been running drugs and guns and smuggling people in and out of the States for months. If it were one of those activities, we'd be out of the loop. But it wasn't one activity. It was the full gamut.

It also appeared that they had funding from some big busi-nesses in hostile places, as well as possible connections with powerful people in the U.S. Homeland tried to take over on account of this. Frank managed to push them back.

The men themselves were a mix of U.S. citizens, Colombians, and guys from the Middle East. That was the only thing that clouded our initial assumption. Why were so many different groups working together? I hoped that this guy, who looked like he might be Colombian, could tie some of those loose ends together for us. Assuming he talked, that is.

"OK, Mr. Noble," the doctor said from the other side of the wall. "He's all yours."

I drank the last of my coffee and pushed off the infirmary wall and met Frank and the man at the entrance. The doctor had set the bone and placed an air cast over the man's forearm. The guy sat on the edge of the gurney, shoulders slumped, head hanging, and eyes focused on the floor.

"Take him to room one," I said to Frank. Then I turned to the doctor. "Can he hold up?"

The doctor shrugged. "Maybe. I'll stick around. I've got a few things that can help keep him up and awake through whatever you do to him."

"You won't want to watch if it gets to that."

"With what you guys pay me, I can watch anything."

"Go wait in your office. We'll get you if we need you."

The doctor held up his hands. He then crossed the room and went into his office, which was on the wall opposite of mine. He closed his door and took a seat behind his computer. I glanced in as I passed and saw the familiar green game board of computer solitaire.

Frank had placed the guy in the interrogation room and now stood on the outside, watching the man through the smoky mirrored glass.

"What do you think?" I said as I stopped next to him, a few feet separating us.

"No doubt he's got information. And if our intel was right, he was at that bus stop for a reason."

I nodded and said nothing, waiting for Frank to continue.

"Something was about to go down," Frank said.

I nodded again, remaining quiet.

"Question is what, Jack? And is he one of them? Or was he there to meet them?"

"Great questions, Frank," I said. "Only one way to find out."

He nodded and smiled. "You ready?"

"Not quite." I took two steps to the right and adjusted the thermostat, turning it down to fifty degrees. "Let's freeze him out for a bit."

Half an hour passed while we downed two cups of coffee each. Neither of us said much. After two years of working together, there was no need for idle banter between us. Both of us knew what needed to be done. We each had our own tactics, and they played well off one another.

I got up and went to check on the man. He looked considerably uncomfortable. "Let's go, Frank."

Frank entered the room ahead of me. He sat at the far end of a rectangular wooden table. I sat in the middle, opposite our prisoner. The man looked between us. His lips quivered and his teeth chattered. He sniffled and shivered.

"Can we get you anything?" Frank asked.

"A coat," the man replied.

"We can do that," Frank said. "Can't we, Jack?"

I nodded. "Sure, but first you need to answer a few questions for us."

The man stared at a spot on the table and said nothing.

"What's your name?" I said.

The man said nothing.

"Your name?" I said again.

"Pablo," he said without looking up.

"What were you doing at that bus stop?" I said.

The man slowly turned his head. His teeth stopped chattering as he clenched his jaw. Muscles rippled at the bottom corners of his face. He licked his lips and calmly said, "I want my lawyer. I'm not saying anything until my lawyer is here."

Frank laughed. "I'm sorry. Do you think you have rights down here? Jack, did you read this guy his rights?"

I shook my head and said nothing.

Frank stood and positioned himself next to me, across the table from the guy. "OK, asshole, here are your rights. You have the right to sit in that chair. You have the right to answer every friggin' question we ask you. You don't have the right to remain silent. Your efforts to remain silent are going to be met with a pain so intense you'll wish we had amputated your arm instead of breaking it. You don't get a lawyer or a chaplain or your mommy. That doctor over there, he's on our side. He can give you medication to keep you awake through any amount of pain we put you through. You won't pass out, asshole. You'll cry until you have no more tears. You'll puke until all your stomach is barren and all you can do is dry heave. So answer my partner's question or your pain is going to start in about thirty seconds."

The man clenched the hand of his good arm into a fist. His eyes watered. I assumed the reality of the situation hit him at that moment. We weren't the cops and there was nothing legal about us. At least not in any sense that he, or most people, understood. Frank and I were authorized to do our jobs, no matter what it took. We could come and go and shoot to kill without asking questions, and without having questions asked of us.

Frank placed both hands on the table and leaned over until he was no more than a foot from the guy's face. "So what's it going to be?"

The man pulled his head back a few inches. His lips thinned and his cheeks puffed out. Frank jerked to the side in time to avoid most of the spittle that flew out of the guy's mouth.

Frank reached out and grabbed the man's right wrist and

yanked up, then down. The man screamed as the jagged edges of his broken bones grated against one another.

Frank pulled out a knife. "The bones are already broken. Shouldn't be tough to cut through. Then there's a mess of veins and nerves and meat and flesh. You want to see what it's like to hold your own severed arm?"

"Enough," the man said through clenched teeth. "I'll talk. I'll talk."

The left side of Frank's mouth turned upward in a smile. He broke the guy down fast. While we'd seen some turn faster, we expected this guy to last a few rounds before caving in.

Frank let go and the man pulled his broken arm to his chest and cradled it with his left arm. He let out a couple sobs, and then wiped his eyes dry. Tears stained his cheeks and settled into his thin facial hair.

"What do you want to know?" he said.

"I want to know what you were doing at the bus stop," I said.

He licked his lips and leaned back in the chair and let out a loud exhale. "Got a smoke?"

I looked at Frank and nodded. Frank reached into his pocket and pulled out a soft pack. He tapped the open end against his palm and retrieved three cigarettes. He lit two and handed one to the man, then rolled the third across the table to me. I tucked it behind my ear, choosing to save it for later.

"The bus stop is where the pickup was going to be made," the guy said.

"What pickup?" I said.

He shifted his eyes from the table to me. "The kid."

I felt Frank's eyes settle on me, but I didn't look back at him. "What kid?"

The man's facial expression changed. The pain and anger lifted, and a bemused look crossed his face. "What did you pick me up for, man?"

"We've been tracking you guys for months. We've got you for drugs, guns, and smuggling terrorists in and out of the country."

The guy his head back and laughed. The spasmodic motion of his body jolted his arm a few inches more than was comfortable and he scrunched his face in pain. After a few seconds he steadied himself and said, "OK, you're onto something with the guns and drugs. They pay well. But the terrorists in and out, you're way off."

"What then?" Frank said. "And what about the kids?"

"Is that all you got? You think these people entered and exited the country alone?" The smile returned to Pablo's face.

"Stop screwing with us," Frank said. "What are you talking about the-"

"Frank," I said. "He's talking about us being way off. This isn't a terrorist cell."

Pablo's eyebrows arched up into his forehead and his smile widened. He looked between Frank and me and nodded vigorously.

I continued, "They're child smugglers. He was at the bus stop today because he was going to kidnap a child."

"You son of a bitch." Frank charged the man and punched him three times in the head, rendering him unconscious.

By the time I got across the table, Frank had backed up. He looked down at the bloodied face of Pablo and shook his hand, which was equally covered in blood. I couldn't tell if it was all Pablo's, or if Frank had split a knuckle or two.

"Well, that was tactful," I said.

"I got kids, Jack."

"I know."

"Christ," Frank said as he stepped around Pablo and made his way toward the door. "What now?"

I followed Frank out into the lobby. The door slammed

behind us, echoing through the room. The doctor looked up and saw us and opened his door.

"Need me to do anything?" he asked.

"Smelling salts," I said. "And check his arm. It might need to be set again."

The doctor reached for his bag. "That's why I went with the air cast," he said with a smile.

Frank stood in the middle of the room with his hands on his hips and his head leaned back.

"You need to get it together," I said. "I'll have you pulled from this."

"I'm good. I'm good."

"OK," I said. "We need to get some more information out of him. Now, I don't think he's going to give up anyone else, at least, not yet. But maybe we can get the location of where they are keeping these kids."

"You sure about this? What if he's jerking us around?" Frank said.

"That's why we need the location. We can verify it in person, then come back and hammer on him some more, and then we'll lead a raid on the place."

Frank nodded as the doctor emerged from the interrogation room.

"He's ready for you guys again," the doctor said.

I grabbed Frank by his shoulders. "Let me do the talking." Then I pushed him toward the room. I wanted Frank to enter first, figuring it would cause the man to feel a little more unsettled.

Pablo was conscious when we entered, but he looked confused.

"Where are you keeping them?" I said.

"Who?" Pablo said.

"The kids."

"In a house."

"Where?"

"Northern Virginia. Suburbs."

"Which one?"

"I don't know the name of the neighborhood. Spring Street. Ninth house on the right."

"Going which way?"

"You can only enter from the north."

I looked at Frank. He nodded.

"Good enough." I stepped to the door and pulled it open. Turned back and saw Frank stop in front of Pablo and lean over and drive his fist into the side of the man's face again.

"Was that necessary?" I said.

Frank looked at me, then at Pablo, then back at me. "Yes."

3

SPRING STREET WAS FULL OF COOKIE CUTTER COLONIALS that sat side by side, a few feet of lawn separating them. The exteriors alternated between white siding with red or blue trim, and brick facades. The target house's lawn was cut close, now a mixture of green and winter brown. Not quite alive, but not totally dead. The entryway was inviting. Christmas lights wrapped the porch rails and lined the edge of the roof. It looked like a normal house and certainly not one that held the deep and dark secrets Pablo inferred.

I started to wonder whether or not Pablo had purposefully led us in the wrong direction. Maybe he had something worked out with the group that if he didn't return by a certain time, they'd take off and go underground or into some state of emergency. In which case, we'd be screwed. And by sending me and Frank out to the suburbs, they'd have even more time to get the hell away, damn the consequences to Pablo.

We sat in a parked car three houses away. The engine had been off for close to three hours and the air inside the car was almost as cold as the air outside. Steam rose with each breath we took.

We positioned the car so the main road was behind us. If anyone entered or left the house, we'd see them. We could also monitor who turned into the neighborhood by looking in the rear and side mirrors.

"Jack?"

"Yeah?"

"Think we're wasting our time?" Frank turned his head slightly and looked at me out of the corner of his right eye.

I shrugged. "Was beginning to wonder that myself."

Frank took a deep breath and exhaled loudly and said nothing.

A flash caught my attention. I looked from the house to my side mirror. A van approached from behind. I nodded and said, "Look."

Frank reached for the steering wheel. The muscles in his forearms flexed as his hands gripped the leather cover that wrapped around the wheel like a boa constrictor.

"Relax," I said. "Even if it's them, we aren't doing anything yet."

Frank's behavior, while understandable, was not typical. I referred to the guy as Ice Man at times because there was no one cooler under pressure. Stress rolled off him like water off a wax statue. He never made a mistake. Not while in the military, and not since I'd worked with him in the SIS. I believed he was incapable of screwing up. But his behavior started to worry me, and worry wasn't a feeling that men in our position could afford.

The van passed us at a steady pace. Stenciled on the side was *Freddy's Cleaning Service* and there was a phone number and the phrase *We've Got A Lust For Dust* written across the rear doors. It didn't slow down as it neared the house. Passed right by, and then continued to the end of the street where it pulled into a driveway.

"Watch the van," Frank said. "I'll keep an eye on the house."

"Got it."

A heavyset man got out of the van and walked toward the front door of the house. His shoulders were hunched over, like a man who'd busted his ass all day long to afford the four bedroom house that kept his family sheltered. I kept my eyes trained on the front door and the windows of the place after he went inside. A minute passed, then two. No action. I glanced to the side and checked the mirror. Another car had turned onto the street and was approaching at a speed slower than the van had traveled.

"Frank?"

"Yeah?"

"Look behind us."

The car slowed as it passed. It was red with four doors and had tinted windows. Our car had the same. We couldn't see him any better than he could see us if he had attempted to look. The driver slowed to a crawl as he passed the house. Frank tapped on the dashboard with his right hand and pointed.

"I see him, Frank. Give it a minute." Despite the calming tone of my voice, I felt as anxious as he acted.

The vehicle continued past the house, but not for long. It came to a stop half a block away and parked next to the curb. The driver's door swung open, but no one got out.

"Think they're watching to see what we do?" Frank said.

"I think you're paranoid," I said.

He waved me off. "I want to get one good look at the guy. If he fits the bill, I'm taking him down."

"We don't know what the bill is. You bring this guy in and one of two things happens. A, someone tries to sue the government because they think they were illegally detained. Or B, you blow the operation."

"Operation? We don't have an operation, Jack."

"Not yet." I felt like yelling at him, asking, *what the hell is wrong with you?* Instead, I bit my tongue and kept calm, at least on the outside. I needed to find my inner calm as well, because both of us acting like jack asses wasn't going to do anyone any good, least of all kids who might need to be rescued.

We watched the car for ten minutes. There was no movement. The door remained open. The brake lights lit up. A slight halo circled the red dots due to a film of condensation on our windshield. Maybe whoever was in the car watched us. Maybe they had called another group of guys and were waiting for them to arrive. Or maybe it was some guy on the phone with his mistress, wanting to finish their illicit conversation before heading inside to kiss his unaware wife.

"Look," Frank said. "He's getting out."

I leaned forward and watched as the man stepped out of the vehicle. There was nothing special about his clothing, which consisted of jeans and a sweatshirt. It looked like he wore hiking boots. He wore a red cap on his head. He looked South American.

He fully emerged from the vehicle and turned his head to the left, then the right. His eyes moved constantly, scanning every house, every car. He stopped on ours, watched for a few seconds, and then moved on. Were we not a threat? Or was he good enough that he identified us and knew not to give it away?

I looked over and saw that Frank had his left hand on the door handle, and his right hand wrapped around his pistol.

"Easy Frank," I said.

"Making sure I'm prepared," Frank said.

He had a point, but the fact was that we were closer to the house than the man who stood next to the car.

The guy closed his door and walked around the back of the red vehicle. He didn't move fast. He didn't move slowly. He rounded the trunk and came to a stop next to the back passenger's door. He opened it and leaned over and then his head disappeared inside the vehicle.

"What do you think he's doing?" Frank said.

"Probably getting his rocket launcher. Then he's going to aim it at us and end our beautiful partnership."

"Asshole."

"Isn't he?"

"Not him, you."

I couldn't help but laugh. "Stop being so uptight. We've got..."

The man emerged, and he wasn't alone. After his head popped back out, his right arm remained. A few seconds later, I could see a smaller, thin arm being pulled out. The body of a small child followed. The kid was maybe seven or eight years old. Of course, I'd always been bad at judging that sort of thing.

"You see that?" I said.

"I see it," Frank said.

"How old you think that kid is?"

"Nine or ten."

I shrugged. Frank had kids. He'd be able to tell.

The man and child started walking toward us. Even from this distance, it was obvious they were not related. The man had a dark beard, and dark hair stuck out from the edges of his cap and whipped in the wind. The kid, on the other hand, was pale and blond.

"Think they're related?" I said.

"Not a chance in hell."

"Maybe he's babysitting."

That, also, had no chance of being true. The kid let his body drop in an effort to break the man's grasp. It did nothing but enrage the man, who yanked the kid up and proceeded to drag him along with the kid's knees scraping along the pavement. Fortunately, he had heavy jeans on.

Frank and I both flinched forward. My hand raced to my holstered pistol and I pulled it out.

"Easy there, Jack," Frank said.

I leaned back and turned my head toward him.

"Let's see where they go," he said.

Looking at the man's eyes, it was obvious where they were going. He had tunnel vision, and the reward at the end of the tunnel was the house we were staking out. The kid still fought and pulled back. The man finally reached down and picked him up and tossed him over his shoulder.

"Pretty damn ballsy walking the kid in like that, don't you think?" I said.

Frank nodded and said nothing.

"Maybe he's had the kid around a while?" I said. "You know, neighbors are used to him. That kind of thing."

Frank still said nothing.

I let a few moments pass without talking while I watched as the man walked up the cracked driveway, his foot trampling grass that struggled to survive in a concrete wasteland. He reached the door, and then reached into his pocket. His hand returned with a key, which he inserted into the knob. A moment later, man and child disappeared into the house.

"Seen enough?" I said.

"Let's watch for a few minutes. If I think rationally, I can explain what we saw. That could be the guy's stepson. He could have adopted him."

Frank's waffling emotions had started to concern me. Here he was neutral and calm, normal Frank. But not too long ago he had been ready to storm the neighborhood.

I shrugged. "Guess that's possible."

We sat in silence, watching the house and the street. No one entered. No one left. The sun was deep in the western sky and long shadows enveloped the house and the yard and our car. The vehicle's tinted windows now worked against us, making it harder to see with accurate detail.

"Want me to call for the van?" I said.

"Let's give it a few and if nothing happens we'll head back to the office and work on Pablo some more."

Ten more minutes passed, and with it, the light faded further. Then the glare of headlights reflected off the side mirror and caught my attention. I reached out and tapped Frank. Tension filled the car.

"I see it," he said.

Both of us hunched lower in our seats and waited as a van passed and then slowed down in front of the house. The right blinker flashed rhythmically, as if telling us, *come on in boys, we got just what you're looking for.*

Inside our car, it was dead quiet. We both held our breath, afraid that any noise or movement we made would scare off the van.

The vehicle turned onto the driveway and stopped near the garage door. The driver's side was blocked from our view, but the front passenger's door flung open and a man hopped down onto the concrete drive. He had on a green coat, but it was impossible to make out any facial features or even tell what his race might be. He faced our direction for a second while he arched his back and twisted side to side, then he spun around and reached for the sliding side door. He grabbed and pulled out and back, whipping the door open. The man that I assumed was the driver now stood at the rear of the van, his back to us. The other guy reached inside and pulled out a child. He pushed the kid toward the driver, then reached in and yanked out a second kid. He grabbed the boy by the collar of his jacket and led him to the side of the house. The four of them walked past the garage.

Large hedges provided cover and they slipped past our line of sight.

"Christ," I said. "Start the car and move slowly."

Frank already had his hand on the ignition, and he fired up the engine and dropped the transmission into drive. We inched along and almost came to a complete stop once we had a full view of the side of the house. We were too late, though. We passed by as the last man entered and slammed the door shut.

Frank raced toward the end of the street and whipped the car around in the cul-de-sac. Again, he floored it and we hit fifty by the time we passed the house again. A stop sign approached fast. Brakes and tires squealed.

"Christ!" Frank shouted.

"Want me to drive?"

Frank slammed his hands on the steering wheel and said nothing.

"First day of driver's ed I remember them telling us to never drive angry. Or maybe that was never drive drunk?"

"Shut up, Jack."

I grinned at myself for a couple seconds and then let my feelings turn somber. I knew what we had witnessed. One man and a kid was a coincidence. A van showing up with two more kids was evidence. Evidence of something I didn't want to believe was real. How had this gone on for so long completely undetected?

"This shit's legit," Frank said.

"Yeah," I said.

"I want to go back."

"Let's do this right. Get a team. Decide if we need to consult the feds or the cops."

"And hammer on Pablo," Frank said as he pressed on the gas and peeled out on to the main road.

4

"WAKE UP, PABLO." FRANK KICKED THE TABLE HARD enough that it slid to the wall.

Pablo had been sleeping, his head down on the wooden surface. He jolted upright, lifting his chin off the table in time. "What the hell, man?"

"I should be asking you that," Frank said. "Who are the men at the house?"

Pablo smiled and shrugged. He turned his palms up. His eyebrows rose into his forehead. "What house? What men?"

Anyone could have taken a single look at Frank and realized the man meant business. But for some reason, Pablo must have felt like he could string him along. It didn't work out that well for him. Frank lifted his right knee and drove his foot into Pablo's chest, sending the man and his chair careening backward into the wall. The chair hit first, colliding with a clank. Pablo's head followed, smashing into the wall with a thud. He slumped out of his chair and to the floor. A long smeared line of blood followed him.

"Shit," Frank said.

"Shit is right," I said. "Better hope he's not dead."

Frank took three steps forward and leaned over. He reached out and felt along Pablo's neck. "He's got a pulse." Then he stood, turned and walked to the door. "Hey Doc, we need you."

The doctor shuffled in holding a half-eaten bear claw in one hand and a steaming cup of coffee in the other. White specs of the sugar glaze from the pastry stuck to his dark mustache.

"What happened to him?" the doctor asked.

"He fell," I said.

The doctor nodded and grunted his affirmation. He handed his pastry and coffee to Frank, then squatted down next to Pablo and began his evaluation.

Doc had it made. None of us knew his name. We called him Doc for his own protection. We all figured he didn't have a job, because he was on-call twenty-four seven for us. I could only imagine what we paid him for his services.

"If you want to get any more info out of this guy, I'd recommend you stop beating him." The doctor took his time standing. He turned and leaned back against the wall. "Otherwise he ain't gonna 'member nothin'."

"Got that, Frank?" I said.

Frank set the doctor's food and coffee down on the table and pushed his way past me and out of the room.

"What's his problem?" the doctor said.

I thought about it for a second. Frank had been taking this operation hard. I grew increasingly concerned that he'd go into the raid with nothing but vengeance on his mind, instead of fulfilling our actual purpose there. The whole point would be to neutralize the men in the house and get the kids out. After that, we'd bring the men back here and go to work on them, finding out the details of their little program.

"He's on edge with this case," I said. "I am too. It's not pretty."

"I don't want to know any details."

"Yeah, I know you don't, Doc."

"All righty, well, I'm going back to my office." He grabbed his coffee and pastry and walked past me through the open doorway. "He'll be up soon. No more hitting him. If you need him to talk, come get me. I'll inject him with something that will have him singing the blues like he was on stage in a dive bar in Kansas City."

Sure he will , I thought. The only thing this guy had going for him was the fact that he led us to the right house. I had no idea if he'd be useful to us anymore. Worth a shot, though.

I pulled the table to the center of the room and sat down at the far end, giving me a view of Pablo as well as the lobby. Pablo started to stir, but hadn't come around all the way yet.

Harris and McKenzie, both SIS agents, entered the lobby. We were expecting six more to help plan and carry out the raid. I wasn't sure who, though. That was up to Frank.

Harris poked his head into the room. "Who's that?"

"Name's Pablo. He fed us the intel that led to the house."

"What's going on at the house?"

"Frank didn't tell you?"

"Wouldn't be asking if he did."

I paused for a second before responding. Frank had a reason for not telling them what we were doing. I had no idea what that reason was, but I felt like I should respect it. "Frank'll go over it in a few. We got a few more questions for this guy."

"OK." Harris turned and walked away.

Pablo opened his eyes and crawled toward the table.

"Hey, Harris?"

"Yeah."

"Mind telling Frank I need him in here?"

"You got it."

By this point, Pablo had managed to get his forearm up on

the table and began pulling himself onto the chair. The man looked like a prizefighter who'd lost his final fight. Left eye swollen shut. Lower lip split in two spots. His nose was crooked and dried blood caked on his upper lip.

"How you feeling, Pablo?" I said.

"Gimme' a smoke, man."

"Give the man a smoke, Frank," I said.

Frank stepped into the room and let the door fall closed behind him. He walked around the table and stopped behind Pablo. What was he planning to do? Strangle him? I held my breath, preparing for Frank's next move. I didn't want to rush to Pablo's defense, but we weren't done with the man, and I'd do whatever I could to keep him alive. Until we had the kids, that is.

Frank reached into his pocket. For a second I thought he was going to pull out a wire, but instead he produced a pack of cigarettes. He grabbed two and stuck them between his lips, and then flipped the lid of his lighter. A two-inch flame shot out and he waved his head side to side. He removed one from his between his lips and handed it to Pablo.

"Gracias," Pablo said.

Frank said nothing. He continued around the table, behind me, and then sat directly across from Pablo.

The room felt heavy. It was quiet except for the sound of Pablo's labored breathing.

Finally, Frank spoke. "What should we expect, Pablo?"

Pablo shrugged. He took a long pull on his cigarette and held the smoke in for what seemed to be two seconds too long. He exhaled a stream of blue smoke into the air then said, "I'm thinking it's gonna be a white Christmas, man."

Frank's face turned bright red. He leaned forward. His fists were clenched tight. It looked like he used every last ounce of self-restraint to keep himself from flying across the table and smashing Pablo's head against the wall, again.

"We're done screwing around," I said. "Doc will inject you with something that will hurt worse than any pain you have ever felt. And as a side effect, you won't be able to resist answering us."

The half-smile on Pablo's face flattened. He turned his head in my direction, but kept his eyes on Frank.

"My partner wanted to give that to you right from the beginning," I said. "But from what I can see, you've been pretty straight forward with us. I'm willing to give you another chance. If you keep screwing around, we'll have no choice but to inject you."

Pablo shifted his eyes to me, then Frank, and then back to me. "You guys are gonna get me killed."

"Not if we get the guys you work for," Frank said. "The guys in that house."

Pablo chuckled. "You think it stops there?"

"I think it begins there," Frank said. "And we'll kill half of them, keep half of them alive. Bring them here. Question them. We'll get to where we need to go, eventually. Here's what I want to know. Are you going to be there with us? Or do you plan to work against us, leaving us with no choice but to dispose of you? You saw how we've been able to detain you without so much as a warrant. I've checked your background, Pablo. You're clean as a whistle. Totally legal. Not so much as a parking ticket. If we can do this, then surely you must realize we can dispose of you in such a way that no one will ever find your body."

I found myself impressed with how composed Frank handled himself. Two minutes earlier he was ready to kill the man, and here he was rationalizing with him.

"Just say you're ready to talk and we'll get down to business," Frank said.

Pablo nodded. "What happens to me if I do talk and give you what you want?"

"Then we keep you around a bit longer in case we need you again," Frank said.

"And then what? What happens when it's all over?"

"I'm sure we can work something out," I said.

That was the best I could offer. The truth was neither Frank nor I could guarantee him anything. Once we completed the operation, our superiors would decide what to do with the prisoners. Some would be killed. Others turned over to local or federal law enforcement. Some might even be let go. It wasn't up to us, and frankly, I didn't care what happened to them.

"OK," Pablo said. "What do you want to know?"

"Start with the house. Describe the interior."

"When you walk in the front door, the staircase is right in front of you. Dining room to the right, living room to the left. The dining room opens to the kitchen. The kitchen connects to the garage on the right and a family room on the left. A short hall leads from the family room to the front door and living room. Next to the door to the garage is the door to the basement."

"What about upstairs?" I said.

"Five bedrooms, plus a room over the garage."

"Who stays upstairs?"

"They do."

"What's in the basement?"

Pablo's eyes shifted and his head lowered and his voice dropped to a whisper. "The kids."

Frank's face darkened a shade. His jaw muscles rippled.

I continued with the questioning. "How many kids?"

"Uh, I haven't been there in a week."

"How many were there last time you were there?"

"A dozen."

"Twelve kids?"

"Yeah."

Frank turned to me. "We saw three go in yesterday. So we're talking fifteen."

I nodded. "Maybe more. Who knows how many they brought in since he was last there?"

"No," Pablo said. "There won't be many more than a dozen. That's about as much as the basement can handle. If you saw them bringing in more kids, that means they moved some. I was supposed to bring one, too. Based on what you say you saw, they shipped at least four out."

Frank looked like he was ready to explode. He placed his hands on the table and inched forward, subtly.

"Frank, leave," I said.

He looked at me, eyes narrowed and mouth partly open. "What?"

"Leave for a few minutes. Get a drink and then come back."

He got up, slowly, and made his way to the door. I waited for him to exit the room and then continued.

"Where do they take them?" I asked.

Pablo shrugged. "Dunno."

"I'm only going to ask one more time. Where-"

"I'm telling you, I don't know. I don't stay at the house. I'm not that far up the ladder, man. All I know is when I bring a new kid in, ones that had been there are gone."

I decided to change it up a bit. "Who were you targeting at the bus stop?"

"It's not like that. It's random. We're not looking for ransom or anything. All kids sell." Pablo stopped and grinned. "Well, some sell better than others."

I felt my blood start to boil. I took a deep breath and composed myself before continuing. "So you've never been asked to pick up a specific kid?"

"Nah." Pablo looked up, his face twisted. "Well, that's not

true. A few weeks ago they gave me a picture and told me to get the kid."

"What did he, or she, look like?"

"He. Blond hair. Maybe ten years old, not sure."

"Where did you pick him up?"

Pablo leaned back and crossed his arms. Brought one hand up to his chin and rubbed his forefinger and thumb against his beard.

"Where, Pablo?"

"I followed him and his mom for a few miles. They pulled into a gas station. It was late, dark. I smacked the lady. She dropped to the ground. I took the kid. But, I can't remember exactly where. I was, uh, not sober."

Frank opened the door and stepped in. He didn't sit down. Instead, he leaned against the back wall, never taking his eyes off of Pablo. I decided to get the questioning back on track. We could revisit the abduction after the raid.

"OK, Pablo, back to the house," I said. "How many guys are there?"

"Five or six at all times."

"Up to?"

"I dunno, maybe eight. Never seen more than ten. If you go after eight you'll only have five or six. And one will be sleeping. There is always someone on duty watching the cameras, so someone is always sleeping in preparation of their shift."

"What kind of weaponry?" I asked.

"I think everyone is armed in there. I know I'm always armed with at least a pistol on me. They have some assault rifles, too."

"How many?"

Pablo shrugged and said nothing.

I glanced over at Frank. He met my gaze and nodded.

"See you for a sec, Jack."

I got up and we stepped out of the room. I looked around the lobby. All the offices were full with agents waiting to meet and discuss the raid.

"Full house," I said.

"Yeah." Frank nodded as he looked left, then right. "So what's your feeling? Is he telling the truth?"

I shrugged. "Guess so. He could be lying, but we know the house is there. We know there's going to be people inside. I'm thinking we should have a sniper set up across the street and watch the house all night. Get another guy up there in the morning. That way we'll have some kind of count on how many guys when we head in."

"Think it's really only five or six?" Frank said.

I leaned in and spoke low. "You worried?"

"A bit."

"You and I can handle five or six guys and barely break a sweat doing so. We got this."

Frank nodded. "OK. Take him downstairs and get him into a cell. No point in keeping him in the room."

"OK."

"We'll be down in the conference room. Meet us there."

5

I LOCKED THE SOLID STEEL DOOR TO PABLO'S CELL AND made my way to conference room, which was located on the same floor. The underground levels of our building were twice the size of the first floor. Half of this floor was holding cells. The other half was split between the conference room and a few more offices. There were two more floors below. One was all offices, and the other had a workout room and our warehouse, which housed all our weaponry. An elevator on the bottom floor could take us down another hundred feet or so to an emergency bunker. I doubted we'd ever have to use it. At least, I wouldn't. I'd always been of the opinion that if something happened that destroyed the world, I wanted to go down with it. Call me spoiled, but the idea of trying to survive on cans of franks and beans held little appeal for me.

I took my time walking down the narrow hallway that led to the conference room. The *whirr* of the overhead fan was missing. The still air smelled like corn chips. I made a mental note to mention to Frank that we'd need someone to look at the system.

And that we'd have to get the cleaners out soon. The situation warranted quick action, but I wanted to make sure all my thoughts were solidified before giving the group an overview, and the time between Pablo's cell and the conference room was all I had.

I stopped outside the open doorway of the conference room and leaned back against the wall. The soft murmur of chatter drifted past me like leaves on a windy day. Insignificant, individually. However, when taken as a whole, it was as if death brushed up against you, and circled you like a shark in the water. That's the vibe that voices in that room had. Everyone in there knew the stakes, no doubt about that. We always faced the very real possibility that one of us wouldn't return home. Not alive, that is. And it didn't matter. Not a single man in the building could say that they didn't know the risks when they signed up for the job.

"The man of the hour," Frank said as I stepped into the room. The group gave me a mock cheer as I took my seat. Frank looked at me and said, "We're ready to go."

A large diagram of the house had been drawn on the white board. Next to it, a street map of the neighborhood had been pinned to the wall. I got up and went to the head of the room and pointed at the house. "We're looking at a minimum of five guys, possibly up to ten, with one asleep." I circled the upstairs. "Bedrooms are here. First two through the door are going to hit the stairs and head up. Next two are going to the right," I paused and pointed at the dining room, "and the two after that to the left. You'll meet up with the team coming in through the back, which should be in place before we enter the house. We'll have snipers in place as well, two across the street and at least one in the back. They'll be able to cover us against any outside interference."

Harris raised his hand and said, "Is two enough for upstairs?"

"No, it's not," I said. "Me and Frank will go in last and hit the stairs, unless things are out of control downstairs."

"What about the feebs?"

"Good question. As of right now, the FBI is not involved."

"Right now, huh? OK. Locals?"

"No. You know how it is, Harris. Both are a possibility. We'll make tactical adjustments on site if necessary."

"And what's the objective? Custody? Kill on sight?"

I glanced at the drawing and pointed to the space between the garage and the kitchen. "The men are secondary. I'd say kill on sight except for the leader of the group, but we don't know who that is. We risk losing information by taking them out. Shoot to neutralize if you have to. If you feel threatened, then kill them."

I surveyed the faces in the room and saw everyone nodding, some in agreement and others just to be doing something. Frank shot me a look that said *let's get this thing moving.*

"The true objective of this operation is in the basement," I said.

"What's in the basement?" Carmichael asked.

At that moment my mouth felt like twenty cotton balls had been stuffed in it. I forced my tongue down in an effort to wet my mouth, and then licked my lips. A thin layer of sweat formed on my brow and neck. Why? I'd been preparing myself since we drove away from that awful prison of a house earlier that afternoon. Why all of a sudden was I panicking over it? Because I knew that telling the group would make it real.

I scanned the room. All eyes were on me. Anticipation hung thick in the air, like black smoke racing ahead of an out of control fire. They were expecting an answer like guns or drugs or a dozen illegal aliens. Christ, over half the men in the room had kids, and not a damn one of them was prepared for what I was about to say.

"Jack?" Frank said. "You want me to take this?"

"No, I got it." I walked to the table and placed both hands on it, palms down. Sweat created a thin, cool barrier between the laminate top and my skin. I leaned over and looked at each man in the room, one by one. "A dozen kids, give or take. Each one taken randomly, save one, to be sold and shipped overseas."

A collective groan filled the room. Faces turned red. Some men instinctively reached for their holstered weapons. Others clenched their fists or slapped the table. I began to wonder if we'd take any prisoners out of the house alive.

"Holy shit," McKenzie said.

"Yeah." I had to control the room before thoughts and tempers got too far out of hand. "So be extra careful when we're clearing the house. I don't know for sure if the kids are allowed out of the basement or not. So watch for little people."

"I'm ready to go now," Carmichael said.

I raised both hands and held them in front of my chest. "We go tomorrow. Get your rest tonight."

"What if they move out with one or more of the kids?" Klein said.

"We've got a man there already. He's watching. We've got a few units nearby. In cars and ready to go. If they try to leave with a child, we'll be on their asses."

The room fell silent. An audible *whirr* sound slipped in from the hall. The fan had kicked back on. Maybe Frank had already called about it.

"All right, guys," I said. "I got nothing else. We'll reconvene here at noon. Go spend time with your families. And those of you still single don't get too drunk tonight."

The last comment elicited a couple of chuckles and grins. The men got up and left the room without a word. After they cleared out, only Frank and I remained.

"I think that went OK," he said.

I shrugged. "Suppose so." I sat down across from Frank. "'Bout as well as I expected."

"You think they'll aim to neutralize?"

"No," I said. "You?"

Frank shook his head and didn't respond. He leaned back and crossed his arms. His head dropped back to the point where the edge of the back of the chair supported him at the base of his neck. His Adam's apple bobbed up then down, and then he cleared his throat.

I waited a few seconds for him say something. He didn't. I rapped on the table twice with my knuckles and stood. "I'm going to head out. Grab a beer with me?"

He shifted in the chair and straightened up. "Nah. Think I'll head home."

"Suit yourself." I walked to the door and glanced over my shoulder. He'd slouched down again and was staring at the ceiling. There was no point in asking again. Frank would spend the night in the office, like he had most nights the last two months.

6

Frank pulled our car into the parking lot of a closed down donut shop about a mile from the house. I stepped out into the cold air. The wind hit me like a sheet of ice. My cheeks burned and my lips went dry. Dark clouds hung low in the sky, a prelude to a winter storm. As long as the snow held off a few hours, they'd be beneficial to us, blocking out the final rays of a dying December sun. By five o'clock it'd be as dark as night. Dark enough for us to move down the street undetected.

I grabbed my earpiece and wrapped it around the side of my head. Flipped my transmitter on and said, "Hall, come in."

Hall was positioned on top of the house across the street from our target. No one knew he was there, least of all the home-owners. The guy was a chameleon and could blend in anywhere.

A few seconds passed, then a gravelly voice responded. "Yeah?"

"What you got over there?"

"No movement since late last night. Two went in, three exited and haven't returned."

"No kids?"

"Affirmative."

"We're going to move in at five, so if anything changes between now and then, you let me know."

"You got it."

"I'll be in touch before we approach."

I changed the setting on my transmitter to only pick up my voice when I pressed the transmit button. I got back in the car and let the warmth envelop me, pushing the cold from my body inch by inch.

"All good?" Frank said.

I nodded. "Think we're looking at five guys. He said three left last night and never returned. Two entered and no one's left since."

"They must shuffle crews in and out. Only a couple core guys stay at the house."

That sounded reasonable, although, with an operation like they had going, the fewer people in the know, the better. All it took was one guy getting caught, and he could rat out the whole organization, like Pablo had.

Two more cars pulled up, carrying a total of eight guys. They parked on either side of us. Everyone got out. The ten of us made our way around the building. I'm sure we were a sight to anyone who passed by. Ten guys dressed in black cargo pants and black thermal shirts, utility belts around our waists. We had radios clipped to our shoulders and wires dangling from our ears. We quickly moved to the back of the building, out of sight. There, I gave a rundown of our plan.

"We're going to make our first move at five. Judging by the cloud cover, it should be dark enough by then."

"Do we want to go that early?" Klein asked.

"I'd prefer to wait till later," I said. "But once the snow starts, it's going to light up the area. We'll be visible from half a block away."

Half the men nodded in agreement. The others stared, anticipation spread across their faces.

"Eight of us are getting off at the end of the street. Thorpe and Lucero, you guys are going to the street behind the house. You'll cut through to the backyard and wait for us to reach the front."

Both men nodded and paired up to my right. They weren't usually partnered together, but I thought they shared an asset that would be beneficial to the operation. Thorpe and Lucero were the shortest in our group, both coming in at under five-seven.

"Harris and McKenzie," I said. "You two are first in and will hit the stairs. Carmichael and Klein, you two will cover them, then to the right. Clear the dining room and kitchen, then meet Thorpe and Lucero."

"Got it," Klein said.

"Reid, Sabatino," I said. "To the left, wrap around. Me and Frank'll be last and it's up in the air whether we'll go upstairs or help downstairs. I'm betting most of the action is going to be downstairs since we are entering so early. If we're lucky, there'll be four of them sitting around the table eating, and one in bed sleeping."

The group chuckled. Things were never that easy. Not for us. Not for anyone.

"We're in vests and helmets. These guys'll be armed. I don't want any casualties."

A hush fell over the group. No one wanted to acknowledge the possibility that someone could die, but every man thought about it.

"We still flying solo?" Reid asked.

"Just us," Frank said. "Local authorities have been warned to stay away. I'm going to update my contact in the Bureau afterward."

A voice chimed into my earpiece and told me that the van would be there in ten minutes.

"OK, van's on the way. Grab your last smoke."

7

WE EXITED THE VAN HALF A BLOCK AWAY FROM THE HOUSE. The angle of the path we took carried us closer and closer to the homes we passed. By the time we reached the fourth house, the last one before the target, we were pressed up against the siding so no one inside the target home could see us.

I reached the corner and lifted my left hand to make a fist. Pressed the transmit button on my gear and said, "You two in position?"

Thorpe answered. "Yeah. From here we can see two in the kitchen, none in the family room."

I looked over my shoulder and scanned the faces of the men behind me. Each man nodded their acknowledgment that they understood.

"Start moving," I said to Thorpe. "First man of ours you see, you burst in." I turned and addressed the men with me. "OK, it's time. Create mass confusion. Disorient them. Only shoot if you feel threatened. I'd rather have broken bones than bullet holes in these guys."

I poked my head around the corner and saw a camera mounted on the side of the house. I had three options. Shoot it, or send someone out to disable it, or ignore it. If I shot it, someone would hear, even though I carried an H&K MP7S equipped with a suppressor. Sending someone out to disable could give them advanced warning that we were approaching. If they were going to get any warning, I'd prefer it to be when all of us were closing in on the house, not a single man sent out like a sacrificial lamb.

I chose to ignore it. Call it a gut feeling, but I reasoned that if two of the men were in the kitchen, they were getting ready to eat. That might be the one time each day that they let their guard down.

"All right, team," I said. "Flip transmissions to on and move."

We crossed the narrow strip of grass between the houses, hunched over and in a tactical formation. Frank and I waited under the camera. The first four through the door crowded on the porch. They knocked the door down and mass confusion began.

Harris and McKenzie rushed inside and Klein and Carmichael quickly dropped into position at the front door, crisscrossing their aim and covering the first two men. Then, they went in and disappeared out of sight. Reid covered them. The sound of gunfire erupted from inside. Muzzle flash lit up the porch. Reid was knocked back five feet and hit the ground. I felt my stomach drop.

"Shit," Frank said.

"Updates," I said.

"Upstairs is clear," Harris said. "We've got one up here."

"We're going in," Thorpe said.

No one else responded.

I rushed to the door and stopped. Frank took position next to me, ready to cover me as I entered. I ducked inside and headed left. The area in front of me was empty. I aimed my weapon into the living room and then down the hall. The living room was clear and Sabatino gave me a thumbs up from the family room. I rose up from a crouching position and looked over the stairs. I saw one man sprawled out on the table, lying on his back. A crimson stain quickly spread across his white t-shirt.

I nodded at Frank. He entered the house, veering to the right. He gestured in the direction of the kitchen, then turned toward me. "It's good, Jack. They've got them kneeling down in the center of the kitchen."

"How many?"

"Four."

Four in the kitchen, one dying on the table, and one upstairs for a total of six men. Pablo had told us the truth.

"I'm going to check on Reid," I said as I walked through the front door. I scanned the area, in case someone had pulled up. Porch lights were on and people poked their heads out of doors and out from behind curtains that covered their front windows.

Reid lay on the ground, wriggling in pain. I bent over and shined a flashlight in his direction. A couple bullets had hit him in the chest, right on top of his heart. If he hadn't been protected by Kevlar, he'd be dead.

"Catch your breath," I said as I loosened his vest. I held out my hand. "Come on, get inside."

I waited for Reid to enter the house, and then followed him in. Harris and McKenzie were leading a man down the stairs. The guy's dark hair stood up in a dozen different directions, but he was more than alert after being jolted awake by trained killers and gunfire.

I went to the right, through the dining room where the man lay dead on the table, having bled out. There was a potted plant on the floor, near the window with a black box next to it. Some kind of watering system, I presumed. I walked into the kitchen, stopped in front of the men kneeling on the floor and aimed my gun at them. "Who's in charge?"

No one spoke.

I kicked one in the stomach. He bent over and fell forward onto his face.

"Who's in charge?" I said again.

A middle-aged guy with a dark full beard lined with gray pointed toward the dining room. "Him."

I looked at Frank, who shook his head.

"Dammit," I said. "OK, Thorpe and Lucero, you two secure these guys. Van's on the way. Load them up quickly once it's here."

"Got it," Thorpe said.

I walked to the other end of the kitchen and into a short hallway with two doors at the end. One led to the garage and one to the basement. I leaned against the first door and heard the sound of children crying. Although I knew this would likely be the scenario, a big part of me still didn't want to believe it, didn't want to face it. I began to reach for the handle, but stopped, deciding to address the group.

"Let's be quick, but gentle. These kids have been through a lot."

No one argued.

I started to turn back toward the door when it flung open and knocked me into the wall at the end of the hall. A barrage of gunfire tore through the small area, riddling Carmichael and Klein with bullets. The men flew backward into the wall. Their bodies were silhouetted by a mixture of each other's blood.

I kicked against the door, but could only get it to move a few inches. I raised my MP7 and aimed it at chest level. I couldn't fire, though. What if this lunatic held one of the kids? I grabbed the top of the door and pulled myself up. Before I reached the top I heard six bursts of three-round fire, telling me that my guys had taken care of the situation. The door moved freely now and I released it and pushed it as far as it would go. On the ground, a pool of blood formed and flowed under the gap between the door and floor. I made my way around and stood in front of the man that had murdered my men. He laid face down, head turned to the side, with his eyes wide open. I lifted my leg and drove the heel of my boot into his face.

"Jack," Frank said. "Let's get the kids before more of these guys show up."

My breathing was erratic and fast and heavy. My heart pounded like a snare drum. "Sabatino, watch the door," I said through labored breathing. I pointed at Harris and McKenzie. "Help us get the kids out."

Although I had braced myself for the worst possible scenario, nothing could have prepared me for what I saw when I reached the bottom of the basement stairs.

The far end of the basement had been dug out an additional eight feet into the ground, forming what looked to be a fifteen foot square pit, eight feet deep. A dozen kids huddled together in a corner. There were boys and girls. They looked like they ranged from five to twelve years old. All of them trapped like rats.

I'm a hardened man. I'd seen and done a lot in my time since joining the Marines at age eighteen, but that sight sent a rush of bile crawling up my throat. I brought a fist to my mouth, worried I was going to throw up. I didn't. Harris did, though, causing a reaction among the children below.

"Don't hurt us," one of them said.

"We're here to help you," I said. "We're the good guys."

Sobs riddled with fear quickly turned into tears of joy. Even the kids that hadn't been crying were now. I looked around the room and caught sight of the faces of the men I was with. Each man had tears in his eyes. Frank's cheeks were stained wet.

"How do they get you out of there?" I said.

A boy stepped forward. He looked to be the oldest. He had brown hair that hung past his eyebrows. His clothes were dirty and tattered. Hell, all of their clothes were. The boy said, "They use a ladder."

I turned and shined my light around the room. "Anyone see a ladder?"

"Over there," Harris said, crossing to the back of the room.

We extended the ladder and dropped it into the pit. I climbed down and asked the older boy to help me rush the kids up. There were twelve kids and four of us. I figured the best thing was to get them up and out in groups of three. I started with the two youngest, and what looked to be the next oldest.

"Harris," I said. "Get these three out of the house. Go through the back yard to the next street over."

Me and the older boy ushered the kids up the ladder. The littlest one was a young girl, maybe five or six years old. Her blond hair was pulled back into a ponytail.

"I can't do it," she said.

"Yes you can," I said as I crouched down so I was eye level with her. I placed my hands on her shoulders. "The sooner you get up that ladder, the sooner you'll see your mommy and daddy."

"Are they up there? Waiting for me?"

I lied. "Yeah, now go."

Her little hands wrapped around the aluminum rungs. She pressed her chest tight to the ladder, stuck her butt out. I didn't care how she climbed it, as long as she got out. She reached the top and the next two kids followed without hesitation. I think they all heard me say that parents were waiting for them outside and that seemed to light a fire under them.

I started the next group up the ladder when Thorpe came running in shouting.

"Fire," he said. "There's a fire."

"What?" I said. "How?"

"No clue," he said. "It's upstairs and moving fast."

Now we really had to move. Calm and careful wasn't going to get us out of this alive. The terrified looks on the kids' faces nearly sent me into a panic.

"You," I said to the older boy. "Up the ladder."

He scurried up the ladder without questioning me.

"I'm gonna hoist the kids up. You four get ready for them. If each of you pulls up two, we're out of here without a problem."

I gestured for the kids to step forward. They lined up in an orderly fashion. I was impressed with how calm they had remained in the face of danger. One by one, starting with the littlest, I handed them up to the waiting hands of my team. After the seventh had been pulled out of the pit, I noticed the last child had retreated to the corner and was sitting with his knees pulled tight to his chest and his arms wrapped around his legs, blond hair covering his kneecaps.

"Let's go," I said.

The boy didn't move. Didn't seem to care that I was there offering him a chance at freedom.

"Jack," Frank yelled. "Fire's almost to the door. Hand him up."

I grabbed the boy and carried him across the pit.

"Stairs are catching fire," Frank said.

"Go," I said. "I got him."

"Give him here," Frank said.

I had the boy across one shoulder with my hand wrapped around his waist. My other hand was on the ladder. I started climbing. "We'll be faster if each of us is carrying one."

Frank turned and disappeared up the stairs without another word.

I reached the top of the ladder and sprinted toward the

burning stairs. I made it halfway up when an explosion ripped through the house, sending a fireball down the stairs and knocking me off my feet. I lay on the floor of the basement. Flames danced all around me. Panic set in. I couldn't see the boy. Where was he? I had him over my shoulder, and now he was gone.

The faint sound of crying penetrated through the maniacal crackling of the flames. I sat up and saw the outline of the boy on the other side of a wall of fire. To my right was a sink and a bunch of towels. They looked like they had been thrown down to the kids from time to time to clean themselves off. Or wipe themselves. It didn't matter. They were all I had. I turned the faucet on and doused the towels, then draped them over my head and shoulders and torso. I leapt through the fire, grabbed the kid and covered him with the remaining towels. I picked him up and held him across my body, close to my chest.

By this time, the stairs had been on fire for several minutes. I didn't know how safe the wood would be, but we didn't have much of a choice. It was the stairs or the pit. The pit might not burn, and would keep us from inhaling the smoke that sought to violate and render our lungs devoid of oxygen. If the house came down, there'd be nothing to stop it from crushing us.

I backed up as fast as I could and sprinted toward the stairs. My thought was that the less time I spent on a step, the lower the chance of it breaking under my weight. It was a good idea, in theory. My legs pumped high and fast and I hit the stairs at full speed, taking them three at a time. Two broke under me when I reached the top. I twisted my body to the side as I fell, so as not to crush the child.

A heavy veil of smoke surrounded me. The walls and ceiling were covered in muted oranges and reds, engulfed in flames. The fire winked and flashed an evil grin at me. It had me. Here we were, so close to the door, yet so far from freedom. A few more feet and we'd be out of the house. Instead, I was down with my legs dangling, and my stomach and chest on the hallway floor. The fall knocked the wind out of me. I was unable to get to my feet. The only way out of the house had been swallowed up in a wall of fire.

Then I heard a loud collective hiss, like steam escaping a kettle. Soon after, water pelted my body.

"Come on, Jack," the voice sounded tinny, far away. It was Frank. I felt his hands grab my chest. They tried to pull the boy away, but I wouldn't let go. Finally, they pulled me to my feet. My thighs and calves scraped against jagged wood. Splinters larger than fingers embedded themselves in my flesh. The pain they caused only served to push me forward. I moved past the men who rescued me and carried the boy through the smoldering doorway. I ran as fast as my legs would carry us.

Flashes from the edge of the yard blinded me and I stumbled. Again, I fell to the ground, making sure to turn so I received the brunt of the fall.

"Let me take him," Frank said.

I relented and let go of the boy. Someone pulled me up from behind and ushered me across the joined backyards of the burning house and its rear neighbor. I managed to keep my legs going until we reached the street, and the safety of our van, where my body collapsed.

8

FRANK HAD RECOGNIZED THE FIRE DEPARTMENT BATTALION chief and convinced him to let us take the kids to the station house. The main part of the building was older and largely unchanged from the picture on the wall that had been taken during the twenties. They had added on a few years back, and the station provided more than enough room for our agents and the kids.

Two FBI agents met us at the station and began the process of gathering information from the kids and contacting parents. I sat close enough that I could hear the elation of the mothers and fathers through the phone as they were told their children had been found. I couldn't help but think of the dozens, maybe hundreds of parents of those kids who had already been sent away.

A couple firefighters made their way to our area shortly after the trucks and ambulances arrived. I pulled a gray wool blanket tight around my shoulders and across my chest. I thought that maybe I could hide by doing so. All it did was draw their attention.

"Sir, are you OK?"

It took a moment for my eyes to drift right and focus on her. She wore blue pants and a white shirt, which was smudged with soot. Her brown hair was pulled back in a ponytail that reached past her shoulder blades. Dark brown eyes stood out against her pale skin. She had attractive features, and I couldn't help but wonder what she'd look like dressed up and with makeup on.

I nodded and let my eyes drift past her, hoping she'd move on. When she didn't, I spoke. "What's your name?"

"Sarah Parkerson." She pointed to a nametag above her breast.

"I'm OK, Sarah. Check on someone else. We had a couple guys shot."

Her eyes widened, and I realized what I had said. This woman had no idea who we were. I could only image what thoughts were racing through her mind at that moment.

That was the first sign that something was wrong with me.

"No, you're not," she said, brushing aside my last comment. "Let me check you out." She pulled at the blanket until I relented. First, she checked me for a concussion. Then checked my blood pressure and listened to my lungs. "Sounds like you took in quite a bit of smoke. Concussion. Mild, though. You got a couple nasty cuts on you. We should get you to a hospital and get those stitched up. They'll want to observe you for the night. Come on."

I ignored her outstretched hand and tried to wave her off like I was swatting at a fly that had annoyed me. "I'll be all right. Check on the kids."

She smiled and squatted until she reached eye level. "We've already got guys checking on the kids. I was sent to check on you."

"I'm not going to the hospital."

"Yes, you are."

I sighed. There was no getting rid of her, it seemed.

"No, he's not," Frank said. "We have the ability to take care of him."

Sarah shrugged and said, "Suit yourself. It's not on my conscience." She stood and turned and walked away, stopping to look back over her shoulder. "I'll be checking on the other guys. Shout if you need me."

I watched as she walked toward Harris and McKenzie, who were sitting on a bench, their backs against a table. She tended to Harris in a matter-of-fact manner, then moved on to McKenzie.

Frank returned with a chair and placed it in front of me, backward. He kicked one leg over and placed his forearms across the chrome railing that outlined the chair back.

"What?" I said, now annoyed with Frank that he'd blocked my view of Sarah as she bent over to work on McKenzie. I leaned to the left to in an attempt to reestablish line of sight, but she'd moved on.

Frank reached into his pocket and pulled out a cigarette. Lit it and didn't offer me one. "Want me to see if I can get her number for you?"

"Hey," Sarah said. "You can't smoke in here."

Frank waved her off without looking back. "Well?"

"Go to hell." My head pounded in retaliation with every word that came out of my mouth.

"Jack, I got bad news." Frank's right hand dropped. His cigarette dangled from in between his index and middle fingers. The smoke twisted around his arm and continued upward, creating a withering fog between us. "We lost Klein." He paused to take a drag. "And Carmichael."

The scene outside the basement entrance replayed in my mind. Both men shot at point blank range with an automatic weapon. I remembered how Klein's eyes focused on me as he collapsed to the ground.

"I know," I said, casting my eyes downward.

"We're gonna have to answer questions about that."

"Christ, Frank. They've been dead two hours and that's all you're worried about?"

Frank leaned back. Had he worried I would strike him? "I'm hurting too, Jack. We lost two guys. Don't think for a second that doesn't affect me."

My ears burned with anger, but I pushed the conversation forward. I saw the night in bits and pieces, but couldn't find the thread to stitch it all together. It was like I was looking at a giant jigsaw puzzle I had completed hours early, only to find that someone had come in and scooped up half the pieces and run off with them. Now I needed answers to put it all back in place.

"What about the guys in the kitchen?" I said.

Frank glanced around, then said, "They're on the way back to the office. Our office," he added as if it needed clarification. "We'll get plenty of cracks at 'em to figure out what the hell is going on. I'm probably going to get the other team on them as well." He took a drag and then made an explosion gesture with his hands. "Any evidence in the house is gone. Burned in the fire."

"How'd the fire start?"

Frank shrugged. "I'm hoping these guys can answer that for us at some point."

I closed my eyes and leaned my head back. I felt the room start to spin, forcing me to reopen my eyes. I shook my head rapidly.

"You OK?" Frank said.

"Yeah." I lied. That was the second sign something was wrong with me.

"Anyway," he continued, "with all the bullets flying around, we could have shorted out something that set it off."

I replayed scenes from the night in my head. They were distorted and disjointed, but I wasn't trying to play the movie in sequential order. I needed something that danced behind a thin curtain, out of reach. Then, I saw it.

"Frank," I said as I reached out for his arm. "In the dining room there was a potted plant in the corner. A big palm looking thing. There was a black box on the floor next to it. I thought it was some kind of watering device. And... damn, I saw one in the kitchen, too."

"What kind of box?"

"Plain. A black box, square, nothing discernible about it."

"So what about it?"

I swallowed hard and leaned in to whisper. "Someone started the fire from outside of the house."

Frank cocked his head and narrowed his eyes. "You think-"

"The boxes were detonators."

"There weren't any explosions, though."

"Yeah, think of flares. They sparked and leaked gasoline or some kind of flammable mixture. Caught the plant on fire. The one in the kitchen, ah hell, I can't remember what that was next to, but I'd bet money it was something flammable."

"We missed one." Frank lowered his eyes. "We let one of those bastards get out."

"Impossible," I said. "We had guys on the roofs across the street. They would have neutralized them. It's more likely someone pulled up while we were inside. If they remained in their car, our guys across the street wouldn't have gotten a good look at them."

Frank nodded. Said nothing.

A quick flash lit up the area in front of me and I blinked hard as I recalled someone taking pictures as we escaped the house. "Photographers. Frank, was someone taking pictures?"

"Yeah. Backyard as we got out. Some neighbors. A couple of them stayed. A couple ran off."

"You don't think the same person that set the fire snapped pictures of us, do you?" Panic filled my voice.

Frank's eyes drifted up and to his right. His mouth dropped open an inch and he pointed over my shoulder. I turned my head to see what the hell he was staring at. The station had a TV mounted to the wall behind me. The picture was on and the sound off. The local news was on. And the topic of the day was the fire. Using the chair, I stood and stared at the picture of me holding the blond haired boy with the house behind us, engulfed in flames and spewing dark smoke into the air like wily, wispy hair on a demon.

"Tell me they don't have my name," I said.

"Someone unmute this TV," Frank said.

A man dressed the same as Sarah, minus the ponytail and other enticing parts, jogged over and fiddled with the TV until the sound came on.

My ears still rang from the gunfire earlier in the night, so I took a few steps closer to the TV to hear. The room started to spin and my vision closed in on me from the outside in. Eventually, everything went black. The third sign something was wrong with me.

I didn't recall hitting the floor or being taken away from the fire station and placed in the back of a van and driven away.

When I opened my eyes and saw Sarah standing over me, I thought we were still back at the firehouse. But there was something familiar about the surroundings.

"Welcome back." She forced a smile, but it did little to hide the concern in her eyes.

"What happened?" I said.

"You passed out. I think I misdiagnosed your concussion. It's more severe than I thought."

I felt the IV lines in my arm and realized we weren't at the fire station anymore.

"Why are you here?" I asked.

"I'm bound to you, legally," she said. The corners of her lips turned up a bit. "At least until someone more qualified can take over."

"Why are you still here?"

"I thought we were going to the hospital, and instead we came here. Like I said, I was your first responder. I had to stay with you." She straightened up and looked around the room, then over her shoulder at the lobby past the window. "What is this place?"

I lifted my head and glanced around. We were in the SIS infirmary. "Somewhere you shouldn't be. Has Doc seen me?"

She nodded. Said nothing.

"What did he say?"

"That you have a concussion."

"Thanks, that was helpful."

"That's what I said." She smiled, then went back to checking my vitals.

I wondered how she managed to get in the van in the first place, much less convince Frank to take her back to SIS headquarters. I must have taken a nasty fall for him to be that concerned.

Frank stepped into the room. Smiled at Sarah and nodded at me. "Gave us a scare, Jack. Doc says you're going to be fine." He turned his attention to Sarah. "Miss, I'll need to debrief you. We'll need to give you a statement and have you sign some papers. Basic stuff, really. In a nutshell, you'll never be able to say you saw this place."

"Don't you mean I have to give a statement?" she said.

Frank shook his head and held out his hand toward her.

Sarah smiled as she glanced between Frank and me. The smile faded, and I assumed she figured out that Frank hadn't been joking. The concern I had seen in her eyes moments ago turned to fear.

"What if I refuse to sign?" she said.

Frank's expression remained stoic. "You won't do that. No point in talking about hypothetical situations. At least not if you want to leave." He wrapped his hand around her elbow and led her to the door and out of the room.

She stopped a few feet into the lobby and pulled away from Frank. Turned around and made eye contact with me. The look on her face was one-third quizzical, one-third scared, and the rest, excited. Her lips were parted, but she didn't say anything. Frank grabbed her elbow again, and guided her across the lobby toward his office.

I watched until she was out of sight. "See you around," I said softly, wondering if it was the truth.

9

THE CONCUSSION TURNED OUT TO BE SEVERE, AND DOC insisted I be kept in the infirmary for four days. He watched over me during the day and a nurse came in at night. She'd been coming around as long as I'd been in the SIS, and I figured we had an arrangement with her, too.

Doc let me leave headquarters on Christmas Eve. I spent the next two days alone. Me and a few bottles of whiskey. Against doctor's orders, of course. Christmas came and went and I barely noticed. My parents called a couple times. Mom, presumably. I didn't answer. I hardly talked to my brother Sean anymore. He was two years my elder, but once he turned sixteen it seemed we were much farther apart than that. I dialed his number a couple times, but never hit send. What was the point? There was no other family to speak of.

I received a call on Christmas day from my old partner, Riley Logan. He didn't go by Riley though, or Logan for that matter. I'd always called him Bear. And perhaps a few other choice words when we were rivals in Marine Recruit Training.

We talked for an hour or so. He caught me up on his adventures in the Marines, working with the CIA. A lot of time spent in Africa, he said. That life seemed so distant to me now. I found it hard to remember what it was like to be tied to a contract with the Marines where I was a servant to the CIA. He said he was getting out soon and thought the two of us could go into business together. He had a few connections in New York who could help us get started. Offer us a contract or two. I wondered if the two additional years he'd spent in the military would clash against the two years I'd been out. I told him I'd think about it. For now, my gig in the SIS paid well and kept me busy. Plus, I didn't have to travel far from the mid-Atlantic. We ended the call after a bit of banter. My mind wandered from Bear to the people we knew and the experiences we had together.

I ran out of alcohol late in the evening on the twenty-sixth and passed out before ten p.m. Woke up early in the afternoon on the twenty-seventh. I'd been staring out the window the night before and left the blinds open. The sun bore down on me, its rays cutting through my retinas like a knife through warm butter. I shut my eyelids tight and rolled away from the window. A loud rap at the front door echoed off the hardwood floors and walls of the narrow hallway that led to my bedroom. I rolled over one more time and swung my legs over the edge of the bed and stood up too fast. Blood took its time reaching my brain, leaving me feeling out of sorts. Another series of knocks reverberated off the floors and walls. I reached for my nightstand and pulled open a drawer and grabbed my Beretta.

I took my time walking to the front door. Whoever was out there rapped on it again. They had to have busted their knuckles by this point. I cracked the door with one hand, and held my gun in the other, shielding it with my hip.

"You look like shit, Jack," Frank said.

Hung over and still feeling the effects of a concussion, I

found myself in no mood for his jokes. I let my arm drop to the side, aiming the gun at the floor. It swung three inches forward, six inches back. Over and over, like a pendulum. "Thanks," I said. "Come on in."

Frank pushed past me and walked toward the couch and said, "Better put that thing away before your shoot your big toe off." He sat down and crossed his legs and folded his arms over his chest. He shook his head side to side as his eyes followed me around the room.

"What do you want?" I said.

"You need to get cleaned up. Shower and shave. Got a nice suit?"

"Why?"

"They're honoring us tonight."

"Who?"

"Some politicians, and who knows who else." He held out his hands. A large grin crossed his face. "Maybe the President."

"For what?"

"The kids. Turns out *you know who* saw your picture on TV."

"Carrying the boy?"

"You got it. He thought it might be a good idea to throw us a celebration."

"Ah, Christ." I poured orange juice into a cup and tipped the bottle to Frank. He shook his head. "They can't invite many people then. Our agency doesn't exist. What the hell is he thinking?"

"Supposedly they've worked up some cover story. Either we're feebs or some special unit in the police. Not sure, exactly. They won't tell anyone who we are."

Sure they wouldn't. In my ten plus years of government service, I'd learned the hard way not to trust a politician or superior with a secret. They looked out for themselves first. Hell, they only looked out for themselves. Screw their constituents and screw their employees and screw the people who protected their asses.

"I'm not going," I said.

Frank smiled. "The hell you aren't. The kids' parents will be there and they'll want to thank us. Go get a shower and shave. And don't come back out here without a suit on."

I started toward the hallway. Looked over my shoulder at the smirking Frank, and said, "Screw you."

10

We sat behind a row of seven tables, butted together end to end and covered with black and white paisley tablecloths. Overhead can lights were aimed in our direction, casting a haze over the crowd gathered to honor us. The attendees sat together in bunches of four or five or six. Their tables were round, each with a single vase in the middle containing an arrangement of flowers that were yellow and red and white and unidentifiable by me.

Three tables lined up to form the first row. Sixteen white and brown faces smiled at us. Their eyes scanned left to right and back again, like they were at county lockup, trying to identify the man who'd mugged them on a dark street. If not for the smiles, that is. Beyond the first row, I had trouble making out the features on faces. And the row behind that might as well not even have been there, because I couldn't see the people at all, only the dull outlines of the tables.

Sweat formed on my brow. Was everyone having the same

trouble as me? Was this a side effect of the concussion? Or maybe from too much drinking?

The lights were bright and hot and hit me like tiny bits of molten metal. Then a panicked thought crossed my mind. What if the concussion was gone and something else remained, bleeding in my brain? That was a real thing, I thought. I tried recall everything I'd ever read on head trauma and its after effects. My efforts drew a blank. By this point, my hands began to tremble. My heart pounded against the wall of my chest. I counted the beats for ten seconds and then extrapolated it out. One hundred and forty beats a minute. I reached for the tall glass of water that had been placed in the middle of the table. The outside of the glass was sweating, and the thin layer of condensation coated my palm. Cold and wet, my hand shot back. A reflex I had no control over.

What the hell is wrong with me?

"Christ, these lights," Frank said, leaning into my shoulder. "Can't see a damn thing after the first row."

I turned my head a few inches to the left. Frank's smile pushed up into his cheeks.

"They better cut those lights when food is served," he said.

My heart rate decreased. The thoughts of panic that clouded my mind dispersed the way steam from a kettle does when it reaches a foot or two above the stove and heads back to the atmosphere. Never gone, only a change of state until ready to be called upon again.

"No kidding," I said. "One of those assholes could be out there right now, waiting to mow us down."

Frank nodded. "Same thought's crossed my mind, too."

A man in the front row stood. He was dressed in a dark suit and wore a conservative red and blue striped necktie. His face was clean-shaven. So was the top of his head. He used his index finger to shove his gold-rimmed glasses up his skinny nose. He approached us. A toothy grin spread across his face. When he reached a spot two feet in front of my table, he spun and faced the crowd.

"Ladies and gentlemen," he said. "Let's stand and give a round of applause to the men sitting behind me."

The crowd rose and began clapping. I felt Frank's hand pulling on my elbow. I looked to the left, then the right and saw the other agents pushing their seats back and standing up to accept the acclaim the audience was heaping upon us.

Reluctantly, I rose to my feet. I felt more exposed than a few minutes earlier.

The man extended his arms to the side and motioned for everyone to sit. Once the crowd obliged, he said, "These men risked their lives." He paused a beat, and I wondered what his facial expression looked like at that moment. Jovial with a smile? Or serious with drawn lips? "In fact, two of them lost their lives. They did this to rescue your children. And when a fire broke out, they didn't cut rope and try to save themselves. No, they made sure every child was safe, to the point of leaving their fallen comrades behind."

Another round of applause swept through the audience. I found it a tad inappropriate. After all, the man had admitted that our operation was a failure because we left our men behind. That had never been acceptable and sure as hell wasn't now. No matter what other outcomes prevailed.

Once the crowd died down, the man continued, "Due to the nature of their work, we can't congratulate them individually by name."

I glanced sideways at Frank. He pretended to ignore me.

"But we can stand once more," the man said, "and offer our sincerest thanks and gratitude for what they have done for us all."

Again the crowd stood, and again they applauded us. A

blond haired boy appeared through the haze of the lights and approached the table. I recognized him not by memory, but by the photos of me carrying him outside. He stopped in front of me and smiled. His two front teeth were missing. One on top, one on the bottom. The light wrapped around his head. His blue eyes stood out like pools of crystal water on a rocky landscape.

"My mom wants to thank you," he said in a voice slightly louder than a whisper.

Frank placed his forearm on the table and leaned over. "After we eat, son."

I held out my hand, palm toward Frank. "It's OK. I'll meet her now."

The little boy smiled and took three steps back. I got up and walked behind three tables. The little boy mirrored my movements and met me at the end of the row. He held out his hand. I took it, and he led me to the back of the room. Once past the lights, I studied the faces in the room as much as I kept an eye on where the boy was taking me. Nothing seemed out of place. I didn't know anyone in the room, aside from a few politicians. None of them screamed terrorist or killer or asshole. Well, maybe a couple guys had asshole written across their faces, but that was a given anywhere you went.

A woman got up from her table and walked toward us. She looked nothing like her son. Dark hair, light brown eyes and an olive complexion. She wore a blue form-fitting dress. I thought it agreed with her quite well. It stretched down past mid-thigh, coming to a stop above her knees. Her hands grabbed for the hem and pulled down. My eyes had lingered too long. An after effect of the concussion, I'm sure. I looked up and grinned and apologized. She shook her head and smiled and looked away.

"I wanted to thank you personally, Mister...?" A curious eyebrow rose up, causing the small square bandage on her forehead to wrinkle.

"Call me Jack," I said.

"Jack. OK. Well, Jack, thank you for saving my little Christopher. If not for you... I can't even think about it."

"Only doing my job." I half-turned to face the front of the room and extended my arm, like I was showcasing a prize package on a game show. "Any of those guys up there would have done the same if they were in the position I was. Three of them were in the pit with me. I happened to be the last one out. Plus, we have two guys who couldn't make it tonight who deserve more thanks than I do."

She looked away again, her eyes flooding with tears. She reached up and dabbed at the corner of her eyes, trying to stop their advance before ruining her makeup.

"But the fact that these young lives were saved, especially this little guy here," I tousled the boy's hair, "justifies it all. And I'm glad we could get together and meet in person, Miss?"

"Oh, I'm sorry." She extended her hand and said, "Tammy Nockowitz."

The name didn't match the features. "Married name?" I asked.

"Yeah, but I'm not married anymore." She bit the bottom of her lip and dipped her head an inch. "So, if you wanted to ask me out..."

I smiled at her then looked down at her son who had lost interest in our conversation a few minutes ago. My smile faded as I met her stare. "I'm not boyfriend material. You should return to your table."

Tammy's cheeks turned a shade of red. She averted her eyes, then reached down for her son's hand and pulled him toward their seats.

I watched her walk away, questioning if I'd done the right thing. Of course I had. I was in no position to be with a woman with a child. I placed myself in harm's way six days out of every seven. It would be irresponsible to get close to a child and then disappear, whether physically or emotionally.

I took a couple steps back and turned a beat too fast. A pair of hands slammed into my solar plexus, nearly winding me.

"I'm sorry," I said, trying to avoid looking at whoever I'd hit.

"Real slick, Jack."

I stopped trying to get away and looked at the woman in front of me and recognized her as Sarah, the paramedic who had been roped into duty at the SIS.

"I don't mean now. I mean, this is cool, too. The way you ran into me and tried to act like nothing happened." She smiled and leaned in, placing her mouth inches from my ear. "But the way you rejected that woman, that was classy."

I stepped back, holding my hands out in front of me to maintain separation. "You don't know the first thing about me, lady."

She laughed. "I know plenty."

I turned my head and saw that the majority of the seats around the tables were now empty. A line had formed in front of the tables where the rest of my group sat. "Christ," I muttered. "Come on, let's get a drink."

Sarah smirked and latched onto my arm. We moved to the back of the room and each took a seat on a barstool. I ordered a shot of Johnny and she ordered a beer. By the time she finished her beer, I'd downed four shots.

Doc would have been pleased.

We talked about nothing at all. The kind of mindless chatter people have when they are feeling each other out. I had a feeling that she had a feeling about me. And I found her easy on the eyes and equipped with the kind of tough take-no-crap exterior I found myself regularly attracted to. I wanted to know if it was an act, or if she really was as badass as she seemed.

She told me she was born and raised in D.C. Went to college at Georgetown, decided to join the fire department instead of going to medical school. She'd been married once, but it didn't even last a year. Apparently the guy couldn't handle the thought of his wife rushing into a burning building.

I told her a few select things about my past, like how I turned down a football scholarship and joined the Marines. Dumbed down the eight years spent there, but let her know that it led me to where I am now. Told her I'd never been married. Lied and said I'd never been engaged. She didn't need to know.

After fifteen minutes I began to feel the effects of the alcohol. My head buzzed slightly. She was already done with her second beer and began smiling a bit more.

I said something that made her laugh. Strands of hair fell across her face. She reached up and tucked them behind her ear, then said, "So how emotionally unavailable are you?"

"On a scale of one to ten, I'm an eleven. Or a zero, depending on which way your scale slides."

"I like that in a man."

"I like a woman who likes that in a man."

She smiled and leaned in a couple inches. "Want to get out of here? Split a cab somewhere?"

"Where?"

She shrugged. "Whoever's house is closest?"

I nodded then looked around to get my bearings and located the coat check. I felt her fingers slide in between mine. Her palm, cool from holding a beer mug, melted into my hand.

"Jack." It was the right name, wrong voice.

I felt deflated. Frank headed toward me, another man close behind. The guy following was older than me, probably mid-forties, maybe early fifties. Hard to tell. His hair was blond, perhaps hiding traces of gray. He was wide in the shoulders and narrow in the hips. Looked like an athlete in a custom tailored gray suit. He had a winning smile and everything about him screamed politician.

"Man of the hour," Sarah said from behind me.

I turned and caught her eye. "I'm sorry. As soon as this is over."

"It's OK. I'll have a few more drinks. You won't mind, will you?"

I smiled, tossed back another shot and hopped off my barstool. Walked a few feet away from the bar and waited for Frank and his friend.

"Jack, this is Senator Burnett. He's, uh, he's a friend of ours."

The Senator smiled his politician's smile and held out his hand. His grip was firm and comforting. "I watch from a distance." His smile broadened and he winked. "And you always provide one hell of a show, Jack."

I had been prepared to hate the man. After all, he was holding me back from beginning a night with Sarah. But there was something about his smile and his grip and his voice that made me feel at ease with him. I presumed that most people felt that way about him. I assumed that's why he was a successful politician. Half shark, half used car salesman, all bullshit.

"Let's have a drink." Senator Burnett draped his right arm across my shoulders, his left across Frank's. He guided us toward the bar. I did nothing to stop him. I found myself liking the guy. At the very least, I saw why people voted for him.

I sat down next to Sarah. Leaned over and whispered, "You sure you don't mind staying a bit longer?"

"I've got nowhere to go and we can always find a taxi willing take us there," she said. "Plus, I'm off tomorrow. If you're too drunk tonight, we've got the morning."

I smiled. "I've never been too drunk."

She laughed and winked and nudged me. The force of her push turned me toward the Senator.

"You guys did a great job here," Burnett said. "Even if you did overstep some boundaries."

Frank shrugged. "We talked to the right people. No one threw up a stop sign, so we moved. You think it would have been better to risk losing some of those kids?"

Burnett finished his beer and gestured for another. "No, of course not. I understand that you had to act fast. Next time something like this happens, clear it through to the top. It makes my life easier and-"

"Jack," Frank interrupted. "Incoming."

I swiveled to the left and saw Tammy approaching. "Shit," I said.

Burnett glanced over his shoulder and stood. "That's a grenade I'm dodging. Hitting the head. Back in a minute boys."

Tammy leaned against the bar, in between me and Frank. "Jack, that offer still stands." She reached out, grabbed my tie, slipped a business card into my shirt pocket.

Sarah leaned over my shoulder and said, "Mind taking your hands off my man?"

Tammy looked at Sarah, then at me. "Not boyfriend material, huh?" She said it matter-of-factly and with no trace of disappointment in her voice.

I shrugged and held out my hands. Tammy shook her head, then turned and walked toward the door, where her son was standing. I'd have figured she wouldn't let him leave her side after what happened. To each their own, I supposed. There was no need to waste time questioning it.

After she slipped through the door, I turned to Frank and said, "I'm trying to get out of here. You think you can handle the Senator without me?"

"Humor him for a few more. He's half pissed now. I'll get a cab for him soon and then you can be on your way."

11

BURNETT SPENT ANOTHER HALF HOUR TALKING WITH US. Mostly praise, some criticism. We took it with smiles plastered on our faces. The alcohol helped. The fact that we needed the man for our funding helped even more. If the SIS disappeared, I'd be looking for work at the Treasury Department. No thanks.

Finally, Burnett stood and held out his hand. I grabbed it, surprised when he pulled me off the stool and wrapped his other arm around my back.

"You do good work, Jack," he said. "Good damn work." He took a step back and grabbed my shoulders. His fingers dug in a bit. My initial reaction was to knock his hands away. But I figured he only did it because of the alcohol, so I eased up. He gave me a shake and then let go. Stumbled a bit and nearly fell off the ledge that separated the bar from the rest of the room.

Frank placed an arm on the Senator's shoulders and guided him toward the door. I heard the man protest that he could drive, and that his car was a block or two away. Frank insisted that he take a taxi. Whether he did or not, I had no idea. Frank didn't say, and I didn't ask when he returned to the bar and sat down next to me.

"We'll be taking off now," I said.

Frank reached out and grabbed my wrist. "Stay for a few more minutes."

I gave him a look, shrugged, said nothing. I had one foot on the floor and the other on the stool's footrest.

Frank gestured to the side with his head. "Let's make sure our guys get out OK. They're getting a bit rowdy over there."

The other agents stood in the middle of a mostly empty room. A couple politicians hung around, but the families had wisely dispersed when they sensed things were turning into a party their children shouldn't witness.

"Rowdy with each other," I said.

"Does that make it any better? You know how these guys get when they drink."

I sighed heavily and turned toward Sarah. "A few more minutes?"

She dropped her right elbow on the bar and propped her head up with her hand. She mouthed the word *fine* to me and motioned toward the bartender for another drink. Who would be the one that would end up too drunk that night?

My cell phone rang, cutting Frank off in the middle of a mindless sentence. The display said *unknown caller*. I picked it up off the bar, walked toward the door leading to the sidewalk and answered the phone.

"Hello, Mr. Noble." The voice was awkward, slow-paced and had a tinny sound to it, almost like a machine modified it.

I scanned the room to see if any of our guys were screwing around with me. Everyone was accounted for. No one had a phone to their head.

"Who is this?" I said.

"Mr. Noble, do you make a habit out of interfering in other people's businesses?"

I lowered my shoulder and pushed the door open. Stepped out onto the street and waited for a couple of younger women to pass by. "That depends on the business. There are some that require my intervention."

"That is a bad habit."

"Yeah, well, it's the only thing that keeps me from smoking too much."

"I'd never have pegged you for a comedian, Mr. Noble."

"I have my moments."

"I'm sure you do." He paused a beat and the line went silent except for the faint sound of static. "You should savor those moments. All of them, for that matter. Because they are running out."

I scanned M Street up to the corner of 10th and back. Turned and checked the corner at 11th and didn't see anyone. The windows of the buildings across from me were dark and revealed nothing. Someone could be in there, I supposed.

"That's good advice," I said. "But I'm afraid I'm going to be ignoring it."

"I wouldn't do that if I were you." Whatever he was using to disguise his voice failed for a few seconds. Unfortunately, there was nothing distinguishing about the way the man spoke. His neutral accent and tone could have been any of tens of thousands of people.

My patience grew thin. This guy knew who I was, which meant he probably had an idea of what I did for a living. "I'm getting tired of this game. This is a government phone and we can track this call back whether you're on the line or not. We've already been talking long enough. So get to the point or we'll be showing up at your doorstep and you can tell me face to face."

The man laughed. He sounded like a deranged robotic clown. "No you aren't, and no you can't. But, I'll get to the point. You and your team of misfit agents, you all stuck your heads somewhere they didn't belong. Two of them died for it. Who's going to be next? I'll tell you. You didn't solve a problem, Mr. Noble. No, you created a mess. And I'm going to clean it up, starting with you."

"You're real convincing over a phone line, you know that?" I said. "Why don't you meet me at my office tomorrow and we'll get this squared away."

He laughed again. "You are not in control, Jack. I'd suggest you listen up if you want to limit the casualties to yourself. It starts with the one whose hair is fair. A little boy, from the fire, you emerged. Intertwined, but the fire could not dine. Now the sins of the mother have been purged. But there's more to be done, and you are the one, who will face the torture of a thousand souls."

"What the hell are you talking about?"

"You've got thirty-seven hours to figure that out, Jack."

The line fell silent. I scanned the street and storefronts again, and then walked to the corner of the building, staying close to the shadows to check the parking lot. I quickly returned to the front door and pushed it open.

Frank leaned back against the bar and raised a shot glass in my direction, leaned his head back and tossed the drink in his mouth. He wiped his face with the back of his hand and exhaled loudly. I crossed the floor and stopped two feet in front of him.

"What's up, Jack?" he said. The smell of stale liquor carried on his breath. "Old girlfriend?"

I noticed Sarah glance back over her shoulder.

"No," I said. "Stop screwing around. We've got a problem."

Frank's face straightened and so did his body. "What is it?"

I recounted the conversation I had on the phone with the man with the machine voice. Instinctively, I figured it had to be someone who knew us. Maybe had a beef with us. Someone involved with a terrorist group, using the riddle as some sort of decoy.

"The little blond boy you rescued?" Frank said.

I nodded. "That's what I figure. But why bring him up? That's all classified."

"Someone we busted or broke up their organization, right? So, he sees the picture in the paper. Remembers your face. Pulls some strings, throws around some money and gets your number."

I shook my head. "We got that picture cleaned up before they ran it. No one saw my face."

Frank leaned back again. He shook off the bartender when asked if he needed another drink. "The news, Jack. Remember in the firehouse? You were on TV."

"I was?"

"You were," Sarah said. "Carrying that little boy out of the burning house. Same little boy who stood right there," she pointed to a spot near the front door, "while his mother tried to pick you up."

"The sins of the mother have been purged," I said, recalling the words the man spoke in a singsong robotic voice.

"You don't think he-"

I reached into my pocket and pulled out the card Tammy had slipped inside it on her way out the door. On it was her name and phone number. "I'm going to find out." I dialed the number and placed the phone on speaker.

"Hello," a man said, his voice deep and dry.

12

"Who is this?" I said.

"This is Stallworth. Look, are you related to," he paused a beat, then continued, "Tammy Nockowitz?"

"What?" I said.

Frank pushed out his hands and nodded fervently.

"Uh, yeah, I am," I said. "This is her husband. Who is this? What's going on?"

Frank leaned in. I had to pull the phone back before he got too close and deafened the man with his heavy breathing.

"I'm a paramedic with D.C. Fire. I'm not supposed to do this, but your wife's been in a bad accident. Hit and run. She's unconscious and losing blood."

"What? How?"

The man said nothing.

"My boy, is he OK?"

"No boy here, sir."

"What do you mean no boy? She left with him. Little blond haired guy, eight years old."

The phone rustled and we heard the muffled sound of the man shouting something to the effect of had anyone seen a little boy nearby. A lump rose in my throat, and I feared that the child had been ejected from the car, his little body lying on the side of the highway. I assumed Sarah wondered the same thing because I noticed her eyes were wide and she held her breath.

"No little boy in the car or in the area. Look, the back seat is crushed. He wouldn't have made it out of the car. I think it's safe to say that your wife was traveling alone."

"Where will you take her?"

"GWU Hospital."

I hung up and placed my phone on the bar. "Christ."

"Agreed," Frank said.

"George Washington University isn't that far," I said. "The accident must have occurred pretty close to here."

"What about the boy?" Frank said.

"The man's got the boy," Sarah said.

We both turned toward her. For the first time, we realized that she had been paying attention to everything that had happened. From me telling Frank about the phone call, the call with the paramedic, Sarah knew all of it. And when I saw Frank's jaw muscles working hard, I knew what he intended to do about it.

Frank hopped off his stool and said, "We're gonna have-"

I placed my left hand between them. "Frank, let's not go there yet."

"You're not locking me up," she said. "I'm coming with you."

"Where?" Frank said.

"To the hospital," she said.

"Bullshit you are," Frank said. "You're going into lock down until we know what the hell is going on."

"I can give you an opinion on the injuries," she said. "I don't think this was an accident and I can prove it if you'll let me take a look at her. Plus, if you need to leave with her, I can monitor her during transport."

Frank shot me a look. I shrugged at first, then nodded after a moment of contemplation. I had no objections to keeping Sarah around for a little while, at least for as long as we were in the hospital. Chances are we'd head back to headquarters after that, and I'd try to convince her to stay behind if things looked to be heading in a dangerous direction.

"OK, fine," Frank said. "I'm going to call us a cab."

"What about them?" I said.

"Who?" he said, not bothering to look at me.

"Our guys? Want to fill them in?"

"No," Frank said. "Not until we absolutely have to. And even then, no."

I moved closer to Sarah. "You sure you want to go along? This might be dangerous."

Her voice trembled with anticipation. "I live in danger. My job is full of danger. I can handle this."

Was it false bravado, the way she acted? I couldn't tell. Frank would make her my responsibility. If something happened, I'd have to answer for it. He didn't have to come out and say it. It was assumed.

The bartender placed three to-go coffee mugs on the counter. "Guys look like you could use this."

I nodded my thanks and grabbed my cup and Frank's, and then walked toward the door with Sarah. We waited for Frank. When he showed, I pushed the door open and stepped into the freezing night air. I hadn't noticed it when I stepped outside earlier, buzzed and preoccupied. But time and shock had sobered me. Now I felt the cold as it whipped and sliced and found its way into every opening in my clothing.

"Cab'll be here any minute," Frank said.

My phone vibrated inside my pocket. I pulled it out and held it above waist level. Frank and Sarah closed in on me and hovered over the screen. We all read the same thing, *unknown caller*.

"It's him," I said.

13

I ANSWERED THE PHONE ON THE FOURTH RING.

"Thirty-six hours, Mr. Noble." Same voice, still robotic, tinny, and evil.

"Till what?"

"That should be evident by now, shouldn't it?"

I said nothing. My eyes met Frank's and I watched as he tried to process the voice streaming through the phone's speaker. It wouldn't do any good. It was only a disguise. And in my experience, the only ones to use disguises were extreme cowards, or extremely dangerous men.

"I hear that Ms. Nockowitz is being transported to the hospital. She should be going to the morgue. Unfortunately, D.C. is the last big city in the U.S. to have concerned citizens. I've dispatched a few men to finish the job. But I'll make you a deal, Jack. Interested?"

I fought back the anger that pushed up through my insides and said, "Yeah."

"Get there first, and my men will back off, for now. But know this, if you try to notify the police, the little boy loses a finger."

"How do I know you've got the boy?"

There was a pause, and then, "Mommy?" the voice was soft and sincere and clouded by tears. And it sounded human, which told me that the man was speaking through a device and it wasn't something implanted in the phone.

"That good enough?"

Frank's face turned a deep shade of red. Veins stood out. He clenched his fists. "Bastard! What did he or his mother do to you?"

The man said nothing.

"Hasn't he been through enough?" Frank said.

The man said nothing.

"Why don't you meet me in front of the hospital," Frank said. "You're obviously tough enough to take on a little kid. Why not take me on?"

"I don't know who is speaking, but you can tell him that I'm not listening. Fifteen minutes, Mr. Noble. Don't waste any more time."

The screen lit up, the timer froze, the words *call ended* flashed in bold letters. I flipped the phone shut and stuffed it back into my pocket. He'd given us fifteen minutes to travel twenty. We had to get moving.

"What the hell is this?" Frank said. "Kidnapping and attempted vehicular homicide. Maybe we should turn this over, Jack."

I stared at him in disbelief. A minute ago, he was ready to take on an army if necessary to get to the man on the other end of the phone. Now he'd flipped? Besides, the guy on the phone was serious as a stone. We couldn't risk the boy's life until we knew more, nor had some kind of leverage.

"Frank," I said, "they're sending a team to kill the boy's mother."

"He said that, yeah. But maybe they're really coming for you, Jack." He shook his head. "This guy has it in for you. Any idea why? Or who he is?"

The sixty-four thousand dollar question. There were plenty of people who I'd pissed off in the last ten years. From military officers to CIA agents to Special Forces guys. I could probably rattle off a list of names that would rival those on the Declaration of Independence. But none of that would explain why someone would come after me by kidnapping a little boy and trying to kill his mother. The kind of men I pissed off had a spine and would confront me head on.

"No," I said. "I assume it's someone I know, though. Why else disguise the voice?"

Frank placed his hands on his hips and tilted his head back. His breath mixed with the cold air and a stream of wispy smoke rose into the sky, melting with the full moon hovering behind him. "We need to coordinate with the feds, at the very least."

"You willing to risk her life? That little boy's life?"

Frank lowered his chin to his chest. His eyes focused on a spot somewhere between my feet. He ran a hand through his brown hair, then looked me in the eye. "Just be ready for anything." He glanced in Sarah's direction. "You too."

Sarah nodded in response to Frank.

I'd forgotten she was there. Every second she spent listening to us talk meant additional hours she'd have to spend with us. I shook my head at the thought of the size of the document she was going to have to sign stating she'd never mention a word of this.

"Where's that cab?" I said. "We're running out of time and we've got a lot of ground to cover."

Frank hiked his shoulders an inch and said nothing.

I walked to the end of the building and saw Frank's car in the parking lot. "Give me your keys."

Frank grabbed Sarah by the elbow and guided her in my direction. "You sure you're all right to drive?"

I nodded. He tossed the keys. They glided through the air in an arc, glinting in the moonlight. I tracked them until they were a foot in front of me, then reached out and snagged them. We hustled to the car and got in. Sarah sat in back and Frank in the passenger seat. He fiddled with the built in GPS unit and set a course to the hospital. Perfect for me. Now I didn't have to drive using the map in my head. Don't think, drive. I repeated the mantra in my head as the robotic voice of a woman tossed out directions. I drove as fast as I could manage. It was a perfect union of logic and speed.

We had twelve minutes remaining when we hit the street. Twelve minutes to drive what would normally take twenty at forty miles per hour. The simple solution was to average eighty. We'd get there with two minutes to spare.

Frank's car didn't look like much, but it was a beast mechanically. It had a police interceptor engine, tweaked to get a little more out of it than the cops did, and a beefed up suspension. The result was that even though I drove over eighty miles per hour through the deserted nighttime streets of D.C., it felt like we were cruising along on a Sunday drive. I even flipped the radio on and found an old-time jazz station. The soothing tones of a tenor sax poured through the speakers like velvet, relaxing me.

Five minutes in and we were halfway there, mostly because I'd skipped through half a dozen red lights. I checked the rearview the first time and saw Sarah's eyes grow wide as she took a deep breath and held it. I had decided not to look back again. Seeing her in a panicked state like that ruined the ambiance the music created.

The GPS display continually updated the time remaining statistic for our route. It said eight minutes, which I knew meant we had six or fewer. We were making good time and were on track to arrive at the hospital with one or two precious minute to spare.

I glanced over at Frank, prepared to share the good news. He sat pressed back into the seat. Face tight. Knuckles white. Hands locked in a death grip on the center console and the armrest on the door. I suspected that if the drive went on much longer, he'd end up ripping one of them off, if not both.

We approached another red light. I didn't slow down. Frank hammered his right leg into the ground, pumping his imaginary brakes.

A tiny smile formed on my lips. Of everyone I knew there were two I considered to be fearless. Bear was one of those people. Frank was the other. I'd finally found his weakness. He wouldn't blink while staring down a gun, would walk into a hornets' nest if it meant completing the job, and wouldn't hesitate to rescue someone in a burning building. But being thrashed and slammed and crushed in a car accident had him looking like he stared down a path that led right to death's door.

I glanced at the clock, seven minutes in. I glanced at the GPS, four and half minutes to go. Roughly translated it meant I was still on time to arrive within ten minutes, leaving two to spare.

I don't know if I saw the flashing lights or heard the whoop of the siren first. My brain mashed the two together. I then realized we had a new problem to face.

"Friggin' cops," Frank muttered.

"Jack, are you gonna pull over?" Sarah asked.

I said nothing, choosing to gun the engine in response instead. I needed to keep the cops on my ass, instead of up it. We had less than three minutes to travel. I had to reach the hospital before they forced me to stop. The hospital entrance was the only acceptable place for the car to come to rest. Short of hitting me in the head with a bullet, they weren't keeping us from making it on time. Frank could deal with the fall out. That was his strong suit.

"Jack!" Sarah said.

"He's not stopping," Frank said. "We don't have time."

"This does add a new dimension to the task," I said. "He said no cops. We're bringing the cops with us."

"It's not the same," Frank said.

"Think he'll buy that?" I said.

Frank laughed. He had relaxed. Thinking tactically took his mind off of the danger presented every time I blew through a red light, like I was about to do at that moment.

I sped up as I approached the light. The faint glow of head-lights approaching from the cross street started to light up the recesses of the intersection, like the sun coming up over a mountain. You stand below, in the shadows, watching the light fill up every corner but the one you stand on. Until it finally stares you down and bathes you with its radiance. I pushed the car faster, glancing at the speedometer and noting that it read one-ten. The cop car lagged behind, as I hoped it would.

We hit the intersection, dipped and bounced. I turned my head slightly to the left and saw the headlights, up close and personal. It looked like a collision was unavoidable. The other car's horn blared. Tires squealed. I watched in the side mirror. Time slowed down and I saw the event unfold in stills instead of fluidly. The other car, possibly a big old Buick, skidded toward us, narrowly missing the rear quarter panel, spun then stopped in the middle of the intersection. I pushed the gas harder. One-fifteen. Another set of tires produced another squealing sound as a result of the friction between rubber and asphalt. I looked into the rearview mirror. Blue light silhouetted the big old Buick. I anticipated a crash, but didn't hear one. I didn't bother to check the rearview mirror again. At least, not until the blue lights began their second approach.

14

By my estimation, we were less than two minutes from the hospital. The cop car had fallen behind. There were only a couple intersections with lights remaining, no turns, open highway to the front doors of the ER, practically. I pushed the car even harder. The engine gurgled at first, then roared with a burst, and finally settled back into a steady hum.

Under a minute remained. The streetlights flew by in a blur. The hospital approached, small, like a scale building on a model railroad track, rising and growing as we approached. I began to slow down and the blue lights began to close in. No worries, though. They'd have to slow down the same as us.

The entrance to the hospital parking lot came up quick. I yanked the wheel to the right and hit the brakes and the car turned and skidded into the lot, narrowly missing a parked car. Forty had been too fast for the turn and I made a mental note of it. I slowed down, found the entrance to the emergency room, slammed on the brakes in front of the automatic double doors. Before the car came to a complete stop, I threw it into park, causing it to jerk and shudder. Sarah went face first into Frank's seat and then slammed back into her own. I didn't wait around to make sure she was OK. Strobing blue lights reflected off surrounding buildings and the sound of the cruiser's sirens were deafeningly close.

I flung my door open and raced around the front of our car. The smell emanating from the vehicle was a mixture of a gas station and a tire factory. I wondered if it would be in good enough shape to leave in. I left the car behind and headed for the covered entrance. The automatic glass doors couldn't part fast enough. I managed to slam my right shoulder into one of them, knocking it off track with a loud rattling sound.

"Hey," a woman at the receiving desk next to the doors said to me. "What the hell?"

I ignored her and ran to the nurses' station.

"Help you?" a plump nurse with red cheeks said. Too many late night shifts, I figured, as well as too many dinners from a vending machine.

"Tammy Nockowitz," I said through heavy breaths. I hadn't run far, but I'd sprinted, and possibly winded myself when I slammed into the door. It was then that I noticed a burning sensation on my right side, below my chest.

"She's about to go into surgery. No one can see her."

"I...I'm her husband," I lied.

She eyed me up and down. "Got ID?"

"I left it in the cab. He's probably gone."

She craned her head and tried to look past me. I mirrored her movements and blocked her view. I worried that the blue lights flashing close to the door would draw her eye. They didn't. I then realized that working in an ER would have made her immune to such things. It was nothing more than business as usual, judging by her casual tone and reaction.

"I'm gonna have to make a call on this," she said.

I sighed my disapproval as she stepped away and picked up a phone. Her chubby finger hit a single button. I heard the word *security* muttered. I placed both palms on the counter and pushed myself up so that I leaned over the top. Saw a clipboard and grabbed it. My feet hit the ground again and I turned and started walking, pushing past a door with red signs and white letters that I didn't bother to let form into words in my head. My eyes scanned the patient list until I saw Tammy's name and room number.

The nurse might have called after me. Then again, maybe not. I didn't pay attention. I lifted my eyes until they peered over the plastic clipboard. It took a second or two for my eyes to adjust from near to far, and the blur faded. The wide hallway was full of the sounds of machines pumping and beeping, drowning out the moans and groans and cries of people in pain. I wondered who they were. Had they been in car accidents like Tammy? Had some been shot or stabbed or fallen down stairs? Or perhaps pushed? Maybe a homeless guy or two who didn't reach the shelter in time and found themselves needing a warm place to rest their head, needles and tubes and machines be damned.

The hall doglegged to the right. My eyes scanned open doorways, counting ahead. Tammy's room was halfway down the hall, by my estimation. Two men appeared from around a corner and approached from the other end of the corridor. They moved with purpose. They were carbon copies of one another. Carbon copies of the type of men I'd seen working private security in every corner of the world. Both men had close cut hair and wore dark pants and dark shirts, slightly baggy in order to conceal their holstered weapons. They were closer to Tammy's room than I was. I started to move faster than them. They broke out into a jog. I started to run. They reached the door first.

I reached behind and pulled my weapon. "Get the hell away from that door, or I'll blow your goddamn heads off."

Both men stopped and lifted their hands above their heads and took a few steps back.

Heads poked out from dark empty doorways, looking one way, then the other. They saw the men with their hands in the air and inevitably settled their stares on me, the crazy person in the hospital with a gun.

"Get back in your rooms," I said.

Most of them did. A few didn't. It didn't matter and I didn't bother to look behind me or past the men outside Tammy's room.

"Turn around," I said.

The men didn't. They did continue to back up, though. I figured they were trying to reach the hall that they entered through, and there they'd turn and make a run for it.

"Get the hell out of here," I said.

They made it a quarter of the way down the hall, looked at each other, and turned and ran, bypassing their exit. They slammed into the emergency exit and fell over themselves to get out of my aim. Turns out, they did me a favor. With the alarm blaring, security bolted past Tammy's room, ignoring the guy who a minute ago wielded a gun and threatened half the floor. To them, I was a visitor. They had bigger concerns at that time.

I stepped into Tammy's room. She lay on the bed, unconscious. Circles of blue and purple ringed her eyes. Two rows of stitches crossed her head. Bandages littered her body, covering smaller cuts and scrapes. I figured there were more bruises and cuts under her gown.

My cell phone vibrated against my leg. I pulled it out, flipped it open and answered it.

"I said no cops," the familiar robotic voice said. "Did you not believe me when I said the boy will pay for your idiocy and failure to comply?"

"What did you want me to do? I didn't bring them, they followed me. You gave me fifteen minutes to drive twenty. I had to speed. They clocked me going a hundred in a thirty-five."

The man started laughing. Short, chunky, clunky. The sounds of his cackles stopped, and he said, "Congratulations, Mr. Noble. You passed the test. I'll be in touch soon with further instructions. Playtime is over."

"What? Wait-"

"And please, say hello to Ms. Nockowitz for me."

The line went silent. The call had ended. I held the phone loosely in my left hand, half hoping it would ring again. It didn't.

Tammy started to stir. Her eyes fluttered open. She looked at me, fear spread across her face until she placed me, and then it turned into one of the most pained expressions I'd ever seen in my life. The same expression my mother made when the doctors told her my sister didn't make it.

"They took him," she said.

I sat on the edge of the bed. The tears streamed down her cheeks and rolled off her narrow chin. I placed my hand on her shoulder. She winced in pain at my touch.

"They took him again," she said.

I nodded. "I know. I'm going to do everything I can to get him back for you. I did it once, I can do it again."

"He might be dead already." Tears continued to snake down her cheeks in predetermined paths.

Already?

"I heard him on the phone, Tammy. He's alive. He sounded scared, but he's alive."

She said something else, but the words were lost in between her sobs, and as quickly as she had woken up, she passed out again.

I sat next to her, gun in one hand, the other gently caressing her arm. The alarm blared in the background and two more men streamed past the door. I got up and stuck my head through the opening. The four guys dressed in security uniforms stood at the emergency exit and worked to pull the doors shut. I didn't understand why something so seemingly simple appeared to be so difficult. Eventually, they were successful with their task. The doors closed, and the alarm stopped, and they turned their attention to Tammy's room.

I sat down in a short backed vinyl chair, waited, thought about how I would handle the situation. I could play it cool, like a super-agent in a movie. Sit in the chair, right leg crossed over my left, gun aimed at the doorway, smile on my face. I'd make a joke about how they could bring me a mint julep or some other fancy drink I wouldn't be caught dead drinking.

I decided that the best thing was to wait for them and let them know I wasn't a threat. I got up from the chair and sat back down on the bed. I had to intimidate them, so I aimed my pistol at the open doorway. Two men entered the room, anger spread across their faces. They looked me up and down. Both stopped at the sight of my gun.

"I'm not going to shoot," I said.

One man nodded. The other was motionless.

"I'm one of the good guys," I said.

One man nodded, again. The other remained motionless.

"I'm a federal agent and I helped save this woman's son and I'm going to do so again."

Before the one man could nod again while the other did nothing, Frank stepped into the room behind them. Two uniformed police officers followed him inside.

"I hope they're not here for me," I said.

Frank smiled. "How is she?"

I looked past him. The cops explained the situation to the security officers, or at least some variation of it that Frank had fed them. All four men left the room, leaving me, Frank and an unconscious Tammy alone.

"Where's Sarah?" I said

"In the waiting room," Frank said.

"Figured she'd want to see the injuries."

"I wanted to talk to you first and make sure things were OK."

"Things are OK."

"Did he call again?"

"Yeah."

"What did he say?" Frank said.

"He laughed and said I passed the test. He also said he'd call back with further instructions."

Frank exhaled loudly and placed his hands on his hips. "I don't like this, Jack." He pointed at Tammy. "She say anything about the accident?"

"Only that they took her son, again."

"Anything else?"

"That he might be dead already."

"Already?"

"Yeah, that's what I thought, too. Why already? Did they say something to her or did something happen earlier that led her to believe this was going to happen? That the end result would be the death of her son?"

"Did you ask?"

"She passed out."

Frank nodded. His lips worked side to side and I could tell he was thinking something through. "You think she wasn't really coming onto you at the party? Maybe she was scared and hoped to get you alone so she could talk to you?"

I shrugged. "It's possible, I suppose. But why wouldn't she come out and say she needed help?"

"I don't know. Maybe with everything she's been through, she has a hard time trusting. Of everyone in that room, I would think you would be the one she felt she could trust. You did save her son from perishing in the fire, after all. She received the full story. She knows you could have left, but you stayed and risked your life for her kid."

"And here I figured that was the reason she came on to me."

Frank walked toward me and came to a stop at the foot of the bed. "Tammy," he called in a soft voice. The woman didn't stir. "Dammit, I wish she'd wake up so I can ask her a few questions."

"Me too," I said. "I can't help but feel we're missing something."

"We're missing a lot of things, Jack."

Someone cleared their throat outside the room. I looked up and saw Sarah standing there, half in the room, half in the hall. "Sorry, got tired of waiting out there." She stepped into the room, walked over, stopped between Frank and me. "How is she?"

"Beat up, burned up, and passed out," I said.

She nodded and took a step forward and leaned over me to inspect Tammy up close. Her body brushed up against mine and strands of her hair became caught in the stubble on my face. Her hair smelled of smoke and alcohol, but still retained a scent of lavender or some kind of exotic oil.

"What are you looking for?" Frank asked.

"I'll know if I find it," Sarah replied.

"What the hell does that mean?" Frank said.

After working with Frank for more than two years, I knew that of all the things someone could do to get under his skin, being indirect was the main infraction. It drove him crazy to not have all the facts and know what was going on at all times.

"It means I'm looking," Sarah said. "I don't know what for. If I find it, I'll know." She shook her head and continued examining Tammy. "And maybe I'll tell you," she added.

Frank waved his hand at her and shook his head. I could sense his frustration filling the room.

"Frank, let's talk in the hall," I said.

Outside the room, he said, "What?"

"I've been thinking we need to get a couple guys down here to watch over Tammy. I don't trust this creep. His guys could be anywhere, and the moment we leave, he could pounce and kill her, leaving him to slip away with the boy."

"OK," Frank said.

"We need to get some security around those other kids and their families, too."

Frank nodded, said nothing.

"If he came after one, he might go after the others as well. I think this guy has an ego problem."

"Yeah, we squashed it and now he's trying to prove he's bigger and badder than us."

I nodded. "My thoughts exactly."

"We don't have the resources locally to pull this off. I guess I could recall a few of the teams from here to the mid-west..."

"Nah, don't do that. We'll have to bite the bullet and ask for help."

"OK. You're right."

"Don't tell them too much, though."

Frank nodded and then looked up the hall, and then back down. His eyes settled on a room labeled *Conference* and he took off in that direction.

I backed into the room. Quiet and undetected. Sarah bent over Tammy's motionless body. Her hands worked expertly around the woman's neck, torso, and abdomen. She glanced over her shoulder, then flinched and stood.

"Didn't hear you come back in," she said.

"One of my specialties," I said.

"Must have paid dividends in your younger years." She winked.

I smiled and said nothing.

"I didn't find anything unusual."

"Didn't think you would."

"Why's that?"

"A hunch."

"Something tells me it's more than a hunch."

I shrugged.

"Don't trust me?" She asked.

I didn't reply.

"Whatever," she said. "Don't tell me."

"I won't."

The click-clack of hard-soled shoes echoed down the hall. They moved quickly and with a purpose. A doctor, I figured, rushing to save a patient that had coded. Only thing was, I hadn't heard an announcement or a series of tones through the speakers. I reached for my pistol and aimed it at the open door.

The footsteps came to a halt and Frank stuck his head in the room. "Jack, we gotta go."

"Why? Did you get everything arranged?"

"Yeah," he said. "And then I called into headquarters and got some bad news."

"What?"

"Remember Pablo?"

"Yeah."

"He's had a heart attack."

15

I SAT IN FRANK'S OFFICE WITH THE CHAIR PUSHED BACK TO the glass window that separated him from the lobby. I leaned my head back against the cool glass and stared at the clock on the wall. Behind his desk, Frank pounded away at his keyboard, searching for who knows what. I didn't ask. He didn't tell. We barely talked, and during those moments when we did, it was about nothing in particular.

Sarah assisted Doc with Pablo in the infirmary. While not a cardiologist, Doc was capable of treating the man. That's why he'd been chosen for the SIS. The guy had experience in the field, running with Special Forces in some of the deadliest areas in the world. And the infirmary was state of the art. The care Pablo received was as good as any hospital in the area. I hoped it would be good enough to keep him alive. We couldn't afford to lose him, yet.

We had three of the guys from the house detained below, and they could offer information. However, Pablo offered us something none of them could. He was from outside their orga-

nization, a part of it, but not really. He could get in the house
without a problem, and they all knew him. He knew everything,
and kept his distance, which would serve to cloud his judgment
and memory a bit less. He had other interests that they wanted
no part of, or perhaps were allowed no part of. Either way, Pablo
was the key to us bringing down whoever ran the ring. And that,
I was sure, was the key to getting us close to the man who'd
kidnapped the little boy.

I felt ashamed that I could only think of him as the little boy
at that moment. Christ, what was his name? I struggled with my
memory and eventually recalled Tammy calling her son Christopher. It seemed odd, that a man could rescue another human
being and not be bothered to learn their name. I was built that
way. Business was business. Everything that happened went
down in the line of duty. I didn't deserve any credit for what I
did. Didn't want it, either. Wish I hadn't gotten it, because then
we wouldn't be sitting up at three forty-five in the morning
hoping that some asshole named Pablo pulls through after
having his heart take up protest against living.

Frank must have noticed something was wrong with me,
because he said, "Everything all right?"

I didn't answer. Watched the second hand sweep through
the bottom half of the wall clock as it made its ascent back to
twelve. After an hour or two, it becomes somewhat hypnotic.

I heard footsteps approach from across the lobby. I saw Sarah
poke her head through the open doorway in my peripheral
vision.

"He's going to make it," she said. "It was a very minor heart
attack."

"Can we talk to him?" Frank asked.

She shook her head. "Not for a day or two. Like I said, minor,
but he doesn't need the extra stress you'd heap on him."

"We don't have a day or two," Frank said.

"Take it up with Doc," she said. "I'm only here to help."

Frank looked at me, and I shrugged. It wasn't my call.

"All right," Frank said, resigned. "Send him in. I want to hear what he did."

"Well, he-"

"I want to hear from him," Frank interrupted.

Sarah stopped and stepped back, mouth open, hands held out in front of her. "OK," she said.

I turned in my chair to watch her walk away. She disappeared into the infirmary. I turned back, looked at Frank and said, "You didn't have to go dictatorial on her."

He hunched over his desk. "I know. I'm stressed. This thing's going to give me a heart attack."

"Don't take it out on her." I stood and wrapped my hands into a fist and set them on the desk where he could see them. "And you better not try and take it out on me."

He looked up, nodded and didn't say anything, which was the correct thing to do.

"Am I interrupting?" Doc said from outside the office.

I straightened up, turned away, said, "I was leaving."

We squeezed past each other, chest to chest. He went in. I went out, catching a whiff of the sterile air that always hovered around his body. Sarah sat across the lobby on a vinyl wrapped cushioned bench. I walked to my office, poured two mugs of coffee and then went and sat down next to her.

"He always like that?" she asked.

"He's stressed," I said, holding one of the mugs out in front of her.

She grabbed it, brought the mug up to her lips and gently blew into the liquid, sending a puff of steam into the air. "So does that mean yes?"

I laughed. "You could say he's wound a bit tight."

"He's wound a bit tight. There, I said it." She smiled and

locked eyes with me. Then her face drew tight and serious. "What about you, Jack? Are you wound a bit tight?"

I shrugged. "Sometimes, I suppose."

She repeated what I said, substituting 'you' for 'I', and then added, "I'm going to be a bit bold here, if you don't mind." She took a sip of coffee to give me time to answer. I didn't, not at that moment, at least. "Would you like to go out to dinner when this is all over?"

"I don't mind, and I'd like to."

She took a second to process my answers, forgetting that she asked me two questions. Her smile returned. "It's a date then."

I nodded my agreement. My knees opened to the side. Our legs pressed together, flesh separated by millimeters of thin fabric. Her right hand fell to her thigh. My left hand did the same. The backs of our hands touched, momentarily.

"So what now?" she said, bringing things back to the matter at hand.

What now? The question I had no answer for, so I told her the obvious. "We wait."

"For?" She stretched the word a beat too long.

My cell vibrated against both our legs from inside my pants pocket. Reluctantly, I broke contact and stood up so I could retrieve it. *Unknown caller.* "This," I said. I flipped the phone open and answered.

"Thirty-two hours, Mr. Noble."

"Thanks for the update, asshole."

The man said nothing. I heard him snicker, though. A robotic laugh, something akin to a second-rate fifties movie about a legion of robots out of control and hell bent on destroying every living thing on Earth.

"Thirty-two hours till what?" I prodded.

"You'll find out soon enough. For now, I need you to show me a sign of faith and goodwill."

"Screw you."

"Let me finish, Mr. Noble."

"OK, finish, and then I'll tell you to go screw yourself."

He chuckled in that creepy robotic way. "Release my men."

Instead of screw you, I decided to have some fun with him. "What men?" Turned out to be a mistake. I heard a smack in the background, and the little boy started to cry.

"Don't mess with me, Jack. You've got ninety minutes to get them to Lake Pine, New Jersey."

"Where the hell is that?"

"Google it. But you had better be there. Ninety minutes, Mr. Noble. You, your partner, the woman, and my men. I'll call you when time is almost up to give you the drop point."

"One condition," I said. "Exchange the boy."

"No."

"You gotta give me-" The line went silent. The faint hum of static that was always present in the background during his calls faded away midway through my sentence.

"Christ," I yelled.

"What the hell was that?" Sarah asked.

I looked down at her, well aware that the tone in my voice and the look on my face had given her cause to be taken aback. "It was him."

Frank emerged from his office with the doctor close behind. His face was tight, twisted, and there was concern hidden behind his eyes. "Jack? What's going on? Did he call?"

"Yeah."

"What did he say?"

I walked across the lobby, hand covering my face. Thumb and little finger massaging my temples. I stopped at the other end of the room and turned around. "He said thirty-two hours. And he said he wants his men back. He said you and me and her, we need to gather up his guys and go to frickin' Pine Lake-"

"Lake Pine?" Sarah said.

"-Yeah, what she said. It's in New Jersey. And we have ninety minutes."

"There's no way," Frank said. "It'll take that long to get to Philly."

"What about a helicopter?" Sarah said. "It's how we transport patients with catastrophic injuries."

I looked at Frank. He shrugged and said, "That'll work. We'll have time to spare. But I'm not crazy about turning these guys over. There's still information to get out of them."

"We're not turning them over without some kind of contingency plan." I looked and nodded toward Doc. "How long will it take you to install one of those tracking devices in one of them?"

Doc smiled. "Not even twenty minutes. Some laughing gas, a quick incision, then sew him back up."

Frank smiled. He caught onto my plan. "They'll lead us right to him."

I nodded. "Sarah, would you mind assisting Doc with the procedure?"

"No problem." She got up from the padded bench and stood next to Doc.

"OK," Frank said. "You two go with Doc and pick one of the men. I don't care which one. I'm going to get on the phone and get a car to meet us at Lake Pine and a chopper to get us there." He jogged to his office and slammed the door shut. Sat down at his desk and started hammering on his phone.

The doctor disappeared for a moment, and then returned with the necessary equipment for the procedure. We followed him down the stairs to the holding cells.

"Still up for this?" I said to Sarah.

She smiled in response, but her eyes showed worry.

"Don't worry," I said. "I've got your back."

"This one work?" the doctor asked pointing at the first cell we came to.

"Sure," I said. I punched in the security code and the door unlocked. I opened it and stepped in.

The man got out of bed and looked me up and down. He spat at my feet. "What the hell do you want?"

I smiled. Then I took a long step to build momentum and kicked him in the solar plexus. He bowed at the waist, head to knees. I grabbed him by the back of his head with my left hand, pulled him up a foot or two, drove a powerful uppercut into his chin with my right. His body slumped and fell to the floor in a heap.

"Save that laughing gas, Doc," I said. "He's out."

The surgery took less than five minutes. Doc used a scalpel to make an incision where the neck meets the skull. Plenty of hair to cover the wound, I figured. Enough meat to hide the tracking device, which was nothing more than a thin tube, made from steel and hollow in the middle. That's where the guts of the device lived. He stitched the small incision up. We lifted the man and secured him to a wheelchair. Shackles clamped down on his wrists and ankles.

I brought the other two men out, one at a time, and handcuffed them by the wrists and by the ankles. We took the elevator to the roof. Frank was waiting for us there. A few minutes later, the heavy thumping sound of the helicopter's rotors and the whine of the turbine overwhelmed the silence of the still night.

We piled into the helicopter moments after it landed. Frank first, me last, Sarah and the prisoners in between. I settled in, sitting with my back to the pilot, which left me facing the men. They glared at me, snarled. I saw the curses they wished upon me in their eyes. I smiled in return, while aiming an HK MP7 at their stomachs.

16

THE HELICOPTER GOT US TO OUR DESTINATION IN UNDER AN hour. The three men across from me didn't move except when the helicopter pitched or rolled. The three of them swayed left, right, forward, and backward in unison, their eyes fixed on me, traveling between my face and the gun I held. One of the men had been sweating profusely, and I could tell he didn't like flying all that much. His eyes were wide and he tensed up every time the helicopter moved. I assumed he had to take a heavy sedative to make it to the U.S. from wherever the hell he was from. No such luck today, though.

We landed on an abandoned dirt airstrip covered with the iced over remains of a recent snowstorm. No plow had touched the soil, nor had a shovel scraped the ground in advance of our landing.

The pilot informed us that we were halfway between Cherry Hill and Lake Pine, neither of which was a place I had any familiarity with.

Sarah stood at the edge of the platform, prepared to hop

down. I offered her my hand. She took it. I smiled. She did the same. Once on the ground, I pointed at the dark blue Chevy Suburban parked nearby and told her to wait at the front.

Frank was next. I didn't offer him my hand, nor did I smile at him. He hopped onto the ground and grimaced. Old feet or old knees it appeared, relatively speaking.

"My home territory," Frank said. He yelled to make himself heard over the thumping rotor.

I nodded, then looked away, then thought about the place I used to call home. My mind wandered for a second or two. The three angry faces waiting to exit the helicopter were blurs while I recalled a time and place that were now as alien to me as Mars. Or Portland.

As quickly as the interlude began, it ended. I gestured with the barrel of my MP7 for the three men to exit the helicopter, nice and easy. Frank helped each man down and told them to take ten steps, then get on their knees. Each man did as instructed, reluctantly. Frank twisted and turned at the waist and gave the pilot a thumbs up. Together, we yanked the men to their feet and guided them toward the Suburban. Behind us, the turbine whined, the rotors thumped, and the helicopter made a hell of a cyclone as it rose into the air. Any remaining loose snow whipped all around us. It felt like a thousand minuscule icicles embedded themselves into my cheek.

I glanced around at our surroundings and didn't see a single freestanding structure. We were in the middle of nowhere. I could discharge my weapon and the chance anyone would hear it over the sound of the helicopter's rotors was slim. By the looks on the faces of the men, they realized this as well. The whine of the turbine raised a few decibels. The rotors thumped faster. The helicopter lifted off the ground and began its ascent into the fading deep blue sky. I figured in a couple minutes the silence would be more deafening than the roar of the helicopter.

A weak wintry sun began to crest over the eastern horizon, peeking through sparse holes in the trees where foliage was missing or pine needles didn't mesh. It cast a dim pinkish light over us.

When the helicopter was far enough away that we no longer needed to shout to hear each other, Frank spoke.

"Turn around, assholes."

The men shuffled on their knees until they were facing the other way.

"Ready to go for a ride?" Frank said.

One man nodded. The others remained motionless.

"It's your lucky day," Frank said. "But know that we are going to be watching you after you leave us, and if you so much as fart in a crowded elevator we're gonna have an agent there to collect a gas sample, then plug your asshole and then arrest you for polluting the environment."

One man nodded, again, another remained motionless, and one cracked a smile. So did I. I turned my head and coughed into my hand in an effort to conceal the grin that spread across my face. I swung my head back around, avoiding the eyes of the men, settling on Sarah, instead. She had a bemused look on her face, presumably amused by my reaction to Frank's words.

"You got it?" Frank said. "We're gonna be watching every move you make." He droned on for another thirty seconds, but said nothing important. Mostly tried to make himself sound like a badass and instill the fear of the SIS into the men. All in all, it seemed to have the intended effect.

We lifted each man to his feet, then brought them over to the Suburban and shoved them into the back row of the vehicle, shoulder to shoulder, hip to hip, knee to knee. I sat in the middle row, passenger side, leaning against the door so that my legs were in between the two middle seats. I loosely aimed my MP7 at the man in the middle.

My phone vibrated against my stomach from inside my coat pocket. I reached in and grabbed it, then checked the display, although I knew who it was. Unknown caller. Robot voice. I answered casually, betraying my feelings at that moment.

"I'm glad to see that punctuality is one of your strong suits, Mr. Noble." Still tinny, still robotic and annoying as ever.

"Ingrained," I said. "Growing up, if I wasn't at the dining room table by six, dinner was forfeited."

"How many dinners did it take for you to learn your lesson?"

"Plenty. I'm hardheaded."

"And you must have been quite the runt."

"I've filled out."

"So you have."

I looked at each man in turn. They sat hunched over. Their foreheads wrinkled, thin and bushy eyebrows alike furrowed over their narrowed eyes. They listened intently to every word I said, presumably trying to figure out what the man said in return. I figured I'd get to the point so we could move on. "What do you want from us now?"

"You will soon be approaching an abandoned gas station on your right. A place that looks like it operated in the fifties. You know, old time pumps, signs with smiling faces in-"

"Yeah, I got it."

"Good."

"Then what?"

"Leave my men."

"Then what?"

"Leave."

"Then what?" I asked again, growing impatient with the one word, two-word game.

"Go back to Cherry Hill and get some breakfast. There is a great little diner on Springdale Road. The name escapes me, though."

"What about the boy?"

There was a long pause and I grew concerned that something had happened to Christopher.

"What about him?" the man said.

"Leave him and then tell me where to find him. We'll be done with this."

The man chuckled. A voice spoke up in the background. Soft, sweet, innocent. At least it would have been if Christopher weren't screaming. *"Let go of me."*

"Dammit," I said. "What do you want?"

"My men."

"Then what?"

"We're approaching thirty and a half hours, Mr. Noble. You'll find out soon enough."

The hum of static disappeared, indicating that the call had been cut short. I flipped the phone shut, then leaned back against the door, scanning the faces in the back seat. They all smiled, presumably at the sight of me frustrated and angry.

"What did he say?" Frank said, glancing back from the driver's seat.

"He said look for an old abandoned gas station," I said. "Like something out of the fifties."

"And?"

"And we need drop the guys. Then he recommended that we head into Cherry Hill and get some breakfast." One of the men from the back seat laughed. I ignored him and continued. "Oh, and thirty and a half hours remain."

"Till?"

"No clue." I turned my head a bit to the left and looked at the men again. "Any of you know?"

They all shrugged. None of them spoke.

"Of course you don't," I said.

"There it is," Frank said, pointing across the dash.

I leaned forward and turned to my right. The building had seen better days. Panes of glass were broken or shattered or missing completely. The pavement in the parking lot was cracked and overgrown with weeds. Bushes encroached from the unkempt stretches of lawn that surrounded the lot. Vines wrapped around antique gas pumps. The old signpost that once signaled to passers-by that this was the place to stop now lay on the ground, barely visible among nature's chaos.

The Suburban stopped, and I opened my door and slid out. I flipped a lever on the seat, sending it forward and clearing a path for the men to step through. I pulled them down, one by one, and lined them up on the rear quarter panel of the Suburban. The bulk of the beastly SUV hid us from the road. Unfortunately, the big vehicle did not protect us from the wind.

"Aren't you going to uncuff us?" the man with the tracking device in his head said.

I swung my right arm hard and fast and my clenched fist connected with his jaw. He dropped to the ground, his body folding over itself.

"Anyone else want to be uncuffed?" I said.

The two remaining conscious men shook their heads.

"Your boss will be here soon." I turned and climbed into the Suburban, resuming my position in the same seat.

Frank turned the key in the ignition and the big V-8 engine roared to life. We idled for a minute, watching the men and watching the road and breathing heavily enough to fog up the windows. Frank shifted the transmission into drive and pulled out of the parking lot, heading east, toward Cherry Hill.

"What do you think?" Frank said.

"I think he's got us by the balls at the moment," I said.

"That's going to change, though," Frank said.

"I know."

"Any requests for breakfast?"

"Doesn't matter to me." My stomach felt empty and my head like lead. I needed food and coffee, and not necessarily in that order. "Stay off Springdale Road," I added.

"Why's that?" Frank said.

"He recommended we go to a place on Springdale."

"You think he was hinting at something maybe? Like you'd find something there?"

"Yeah," I said. "A bullet to the back of the head."

Frank chuckled the way that only a man who'd done the things we'd done, and seen the things we'd seen, could.

We drove for twenty minutes and found a place on the northern outskirts of the city. I leaned over and got a look at the clock in the dash. Almost six a.m. Almost thirty hours remaining. I laughed at the fact that I'd threatened myself. Only I didn't know why.

17

WE TOOK A BOOTH IN THE BACK CORNER OF THE DINER. I
sat so that I had a view of the restaurant, the front door, and the
parking lot. The only thing missing was the entrance to the
kitchen. Sarah sat across from me and had that covered. When
Frank returned from washing up in the restroom, he sat next
to me.

We had a laptop computer set up in the middle of the table,
facing the window so that all three of us could see it. The
computer ran a special program that linked up with the tracking
device installed in the man's neck. I had no idea how it worked,
and when Frank tried to explain something about GPS tracking,
I waved him off. All I cared about was whether it would track
the man with any measure of accuracy. And based on experiences, I knew it could.

We picked them up as they hit I-295, northbound. They
stayed on the interstate for twenty minutes or so, then exited
onto a major road. They stuck to main roads for another ten

miles. A few more turns and they were driving through a stretch of map that didn't have a road that registered with our program.

Frank leaned over the table, his eyebrows hunched over squinting eyes. He reached for the laptop and pulled it close to get a better look at where they were heading, I assumed. This was his home territory, after all.

"What do you think?" I said.

He shrugged. "No idea where they're going."

"Maybe they have a house out there?" Sarah said, half statement, half question. This wasn't her specialty, so I figured she felt a little out of place or a little intimidated.

"Possibly," I said. "Let's give it a bit and see."

They drove until they were deep in the country. North of a place called Hopewell and west of Princeton. Then the dot on the screen stopped. It remained still for five minutes, then ten. Ten turned into thirty.

"I think we got them," Frank said.

I pulled out my phone and dialed Harris. He answered on the second ring.

"When's the last time you checked up on Tammy Nockowitz?" I asked.

"About fifteen minutes ago," he said.

"And?"

"I went myself, Jack. She's fine. Doing well. Healing up. We got two guys there and there'll be a shift change at ten a.m."

"OK."

"How are things up there?"

"OK. I think we have their location."

"Great," he said. "Say the word and we're there."

"OK, will do." I ended the call and placed the phone on the table in front of the computer.

"Everything OK with the woman?" Sarah asked.

"Yeah," I said. "She's fine."

The waitress came by and refilled our coffee. For the first time in twenty minutes, I looked away from the computer screen and noticed that the crowd in the diner had thickened. The breakfast crowd, consisting of people in too much of a rush to enjoy the bacon and eggs and pancakes they scarfed down. A crowd could be beneficial at times. This wasn't one of those times, though, and I found myself not wanting to be inside the diner much longer.

Frank must have felt the same way, because he said we needed to get ready to move and he tried to flag down our waitress. The woman noticed him and nodded. She was busy with a half dozen new tables. I wondered how long it would take her to bring our check.

My phone lit up with a new call. The vibrations caused it to dance across the surface of the table, away from me. I grabbed it, flipped it over, and looked at the display. *Unknown caller*, my new best friend.

"Did you think I wouldn't notice?"

Two things struck me at that moment. First, the voice wasn't disguised. I recognized it, somehow, from somewhere. I couldn't place it though. Of course, it could have been my mind working against me. With six billion people in the world, there's bound to be some crossover in things such as looks and the way a voice sounds. I recalled the blip during an earlier call when the machine momentarily allowed his real voice to filter through the phone line. I decided I couldn't dwell on it, at least, not yet. The second thing that struck me was that the man had likely discovered our tracking device, and that was the real reason it stopped moving.

Frank leaned in toward me, angling his head. Trying to listen in, I figured.

"I'm not sure what you're talking about." I said, calm and controlled.

"The device, you idiot. You think I wouldn't notice?"

I didn't reply. Instead, I swallowed hard and tried to think of a way to control the situation.

The line went silent and I pulled the phone away from my head to confirm that we were still connected. When I saw we were, I said, "You didn't leave us much choice-"

"Oh, shut up, Noble. You can reclaim your device whenever you want, if you've got the sack for it."

"All right."

"By the way, the boy will pay for this screw up. You might be picking him up along with the device."

This time there was no sweet, innocent voice in the background disguised by pain and anguish. There was nothing but the heavy breathing and the occasional sound of sandpaper as his stubble scraped against the mouthpiece of his phone. Then I heard a gunshot, and then the line went completely silent.

I stared at the cell phone's screen. The words *call ended* flashed repeatedly in bold white letters. My eyes drifted to the upper right corner of the display and settled on the time. Eight a.m. "Twenty-eight hours to go," I said.

"What the hell happened?" Frank said.

His words hung in the air in front of me as I processed what I'd heard. An angry man called me. He caught us with our pants down. He told me to reclaim my property and said there might be a parting gift of sorts there. Then silence followed by frustration. And a gun shot.

"Jack?"

I looked at Frank and shook my head. "They found the device. Said we should go get it. Then he shot someone." I swallowed hard, and then took a drink. "After he threatened the little boy's life."

Frank's face went slack, then turned red. He leaned forward and slammed a clenched fist against the table. "Son of a bitch," he said, a little too loud. The heads of several patrons of the restaurant whipped around, and they were looking in our direction. Eyes peered at us. Ears opened, hoping to catch a glimpse of the conversation that had elicited such a violent response. Violent for a normal person, that is.

"Let's get moving," I said.

"OK," Frank said.

"OK," Sarah said.

"Not you," I said, turning toward Sarah. "This is too dangerous. I have no idea what we're going to find when we get to that dot." I gestured toward the map on the computer screen.

"There could be a hurt child there," she said. "You need me."

"I'll call an ambulance."

"No you won't. You don't want the attention if something went bad. You don't want to have to answer those questions. Not now. You're not calling anybody." She leaned over the table and poked her finger into my sternum, like a cop does when he wants to make a point.

"Let's bring her, Jack," Frank said.

Surprised by Frank's relenting, I nodded in agreement. Part of me didn't want to have to watch her back and protect her, which would ultimately require me to drop my own guard a bit. But part of me was glad to have her along.

18

THE DRIVE TOOK HALF AN HOUR, MAYBE LONGER. I DIDN'T bother to look at the clock. My mind raced through at least twenty different scenarios that boiled down to two possible outcomes. Either the boy was there, or he wasn't. I couldn't plan my next move without knowing that critical piece of information.

We exited I-295 near Trenton after about twenty minutes driving. Spent another ten miles on a country road. Turned off, headed down a snow-covered dirt road.

"Next turn is the last one," Sarah said from the back seat. She had the laptop and had managed to follow our progress along the map. Left out the guesswork, which was fine with me. I didn't want any guesswork today. Clear-cut, black and white, give it to me straight.

Frank turned right at the appearance of another dirt or gravel road. Couldn't tell with all the snow, only knew it was something other than asphalt by the crunch the tires made. The sound indicated that under the blanket of white was a road that man had hastily created.

"Couple hundred feet and we're there," Sarah said.

I strained to look past the barrier of evergreens. Noticed what could have been a driveway connected to the road. Red and blue lights blinked in between the trees.

Apparently, Frank saw it too. "What the hell is that?" he said.

I shook my head. "Someone beat us here. Somebody heard the gunshot. Called the cops."

"Dammit," Frank said. "Why can't anything..."

I turned toward him, waiting for him to continue. He sat there with his mouth open, then cranked his jaw shut and shook his head. The SUV dipped and bounced in ruts hidden by the snow cover as he turned onto the driveway. We continued to bounce and rock and sway, side to side, up and down. If the road we drove in on was a suspension's bad dream, then this driveway was its nightmare. Packed snow continued to hide some of the peaks and valleys and ruts, but not all. Frank tried to swerve around the ones we could see, which only resulted in us hitting another. It would have made sense to slow down. But not knowing whether the boy lay injured or dead helped us cast sense aside.

We turned hard to the right and pulled around the tree barrier. We saw a cruiser and an SUV, both with stenciled gold stars on their doors and the name of their police department. I didn't bother to stop and look. Two men stood outside a worn and weathered wooden building. Blue and red lights bounced off the structure, highlighting planks of wood that were anything but uniform. They were lined up randomly. Quarter inch gaps had been formed by years of humidity and hot and cold and rain and snow. The elements had caused the wood to expand, contract, bow, and bend. The result was a structure worthy of condemnation if there has been a building inspector within thirty miles of the place.

One of the officers raised his hand. He was short and wide with a formidable gut protruding out and hanging over his belt. The other cop was tall and lean with a leathery face that, much like the barn, had spent too much time out in the elements. He clutched a rifle close to his chest.

"You deal with the cops," I said. "I'm getting inside that barn."

Frank opened his door, stepped out, walked around the front of the Suburban. He held his hands in the air. He clutched his SIS ID in his left hand. I heard him shout something to the men. The guy with the gun dropped his hand. The tall guy lowered his weapon and aimed it at the ground.

"Ready?" I said.

"Yeah," Sarah said.

I opened my door first then took two steps back and then opened her door. She stepped out. I shielded her with my body in case there were more surprises. Turned out, there were.

A third cop emerged from the barn, coughing and gagging. He made it ten or fifteen feet and stopped, which placed him about ten or fifteen feet away from me. If I'd been any closer, I could have identified his lunch, because he proceeded to bend over and vomit. Then he stood and wiped his mouth with his sleeve, only to throw up again.

Things weren't looking good for Christopher Nockowitz.

"What's in there?" I said to the guy.

He stood there, hands on his knees, bent at the waist, breathing heavily. His head rose up and he opened his mouth to speak, but he didn't get a word out. He couldn't. It appeared to me that he'd had a large breakfast. After he finished, he lifted his head again, and said, "Sorry. It's... Oh, God." He bent over once more.

I didn't stand around long enough to find out what

happened. I grabbed Sarah by the hand and pulled her to the right, taking a wide berth around the unfortunate cop. We stopped at the door. I looked at the tall guy and said, "Why are you guys here?"

"Someone heard a gunshot," he said.

I knew it.

"Then," he continued, "Someone phoned in a bomb threat."

"Bomb threat?" I didn't see that coming.

"Yeah."

"Why would anyone care about a bomb threat out here?"

The man straightened up and shuffled his rifle in his hands. The barrel bounced up and down and settled in a few feet from my mid-section. Apparently, they take their bomb threats very seriously in the country.

"You looking for trouble, son?"

I felt Sarah grip my elbow. "No, sir," I said. "One more question, though."

He narrowed his eyes, looked down, then back up. "What?"

"Who's that guy?" I nodded toward the man still heaving in the snow.

"Bomb squad."

"You been inside the barn?"

"No."

"Why not? The bomb?"

He shrugged and gestured with his head toward the dark opening to the structure. "You smell that?"

"What?"

"Death."

I nodded, turned, and stepped inside the barn. The air felt warmer, but only by a few degrees. No wind, though, which made a difference when the temperature was below freezing.

The barn had the smell of death, as the officer noted. It also had the faded odor of gunpowder.

"We need a flashlight," Sarah said.

I scanned the room, my eyes coming to rest on a bale of hay stacked six feet high. "No, we don't."

"Why not?"

"The boy's not here."

"How do you know?"

"Guess I don't for sure, but we could always ask that guy." I stretched my arm and pointed toward the hay. Perched atop was a head, and only a head. And the head belonged to the man we planted the tracking device in. "Although, I guess we could use a flashlight to see if the rest of his body is in here."

Sarah groaned and backed up. I heard her bang against the barn door as she stepped through the opening. She asked for a flashlight and returned less than a minute later, casting an artificial beam of light into the darkest corners of the barn. The rest of the man's body wasn't far from his head. As far as I could tell, only his head had been severed.

I walked over to the makeshift altar and inspected it from all sides. They had sliced the back of the guy's head open and removed the tracking device. They'd placed it a few inches to the left, on top of the hay, in plain sight.

I walked toward the open doorway, taking Sarah's hand along the way. We stepped outside where Frank was waiting for us.

"Well?" he said.

"The boy isn't there," I said.

Frank sighed and let his head drop a few inches. "That's a relief. You find the tracking device."

I nodded.

"Where is it?"

"You can go in and see for yourself." I flipped the flashlight around in my palm, extending the handle toward him. He snatched it and brushed past me.

A moment passed, then two. I saw the cops standing by their cruiser. They quickly averted their eyes when they saw me look in their direction.

"Sweet mother of Jesus," Frank said. "What the hell?"

I waited for him to return from the barn and then I gave him my thoughts. "I'm guessing they figured if we put a tracking device in the back of his head, we might have put one somewhere else."

"Why kill him? Why not leave him on the side of the road?"

I shrugged. "He couldn't be trusted anymore, not if he let us insert a tracking device in his head. Maybe the guy knew too much, like where they were going and why they were going there."

"I suppose," Frank said.

"It's what I would have done, if I were so inclined to be involved in such an illegal endeavor."

"Half of what we do would be classified as illegal."

"Better watch your back then." I smiled. Frank didn't. Bad joke, I supposed.

"Why so brutally?" Sarah asked.

"Fear," I said. "It's a message."

"For us?" she said.

"Partly. And for his own guys."

My phone rang loudly. I had taken it off vibrate on the way out here. I looked at the display. It was him. I glanced at the clock in the corner of the display. Almost nine a.m. I flipped the phone open and answered, "Twenty-seven hours."

"Your math skills are exceptional, Mr. Noble." Normal voice, calm tone.

"What happened to the robot voice?"

"I deemed that unnecessary. Besides, you don't know me."

Then why did you make a point of saying that?

"You're probably right," I said.

"I know I'm right," he said.

"So what now?"

"What now," he repeated. "Well, first let me tell you that if you pull another stunt like that, it will be the boy's head you find next time."

"You keep threatening me with the boy's life," I said. "Sooner or later I'm going to tell you I don't give a shit. Your game is getting old."

"Twenty-seven hours," he said, almost humming it.

"What the hell happens in twenty-seven hours?" I yelled into the phone, loud enough that it got the attention of the three cops. They perked up, leaned forward, then tried to act like they weren't listening. I took a few steps toward the far end of the barn.

"You'll find out soon enough."

The line went to dead air. I moved to throw my phone against the old wooden planks of the barn. Stopped mid pitch and yelled.

"Jesus, Jack," Frank said. "Get a hold of yourself, man. We gotta stay in control here."

I shoved the phone back in my pocket and started toward the Suburban. The tall cop met me at the door. We stood there, eye to eye, not a word spoken between us. For a second I had a feeling he was about to arrest me. Why? I had no idea. A sad smile formed on his lips and took a step back.

"I became a cop after my boy was abducted and killed," he said.

I looked over my shoulder at Frank, who nodded. He'd told them what was going on, which demonstrated a lot of faith on his part. Alternatively, maybe he had no choice if he wanted to keep this under wraps. I feared it wouldn't stay that way for long.

"Sorry for your loss," I said.

He nodded. Smile faded. "If you get these guys," he paused a beat, "when you get these guys, make sure they suffer."

"Will do." I opened the rear passenger door and waited for Sarah to climb in, then I pulled the front door open and slid into the passenger seat, slamming the door behind me. As soon as Frank was in his seat and had the door closed, I said, "What the hell did you tell them?"

"Enough to get us out of there, Jack." He turned the key and fired up the big V-8 engine again. "And they're going to walk away from here. Say they found nothing. And our guys are going to show up in a little bit and scrub this site clean, after gathering all the evidence, of course."

"Of course," I said.

He backed the SUV up, whipped it around and drove back the way we came. We hit pavement and headed north.

"Where are we going?" I said.

"Newark."

"Why Newark?" Sarah asked.

"We have a field office there," Frank replied.

"OK," she said. "But again, why Newark?"

"Outside of New York, close to Philly, close to airports. A big enough city, but far enough away from the big ones, allowing us to operate out of sight when we need to."

She shrugged. "OK, I guess. Still don't know why anyone would want to base themselves out of Newark."

Frank laughed and turned his head toward me. "I like her," he said.

Me too, I thought.

19

Halfway to Newark our plans changed. Harris called and said that Tammy Nockowitz was up and coherent and seemed to be holding something back when he questioned her, but he couldn't quite figure out what.

Frank got on the phone and arranged for a private jet to be ready for us at Princeton Airport. We doubled back the way we came, which was no big deal except that we were working under obvious time constraints.

We boarded and were in the air by ten a.m. Twenty-six hours to go. I left my cell switched on and waited for a call from the man to confirm it. He didn't.

I sat next to Sarah. Frank sat across from us, facing us. "What's on your mind?" he said.

"I don't get why he wants the boy. Why Christopher? Of all the kids, why him?"

"We've been over this, Jack."

We had, but that didn't erase the question from my mind.

"He saw you," Frank said. "The two of you, emerging from

the house. The pictures of you and the fire. Whether he saw it on the news or saw a picture of you, that's why. He got the boy, and he's got you." Frank paused a moment. "I mean, he's got us."

"At some point it's only going to be me," I said.

"Not if I can help it."

I shrugged. He could talk all he wanted. Facts were facts. The guy called me. He spoke to me. He wanted me. In the end, this would boil down to the two of us. And anyone else he had on his side.

"Back to the guy," Frank said. "He's embarrassed and he's pissed. He knew how to reach you, which means he knows you."

"How?" I said. "He doesn't disguise his voice anymore. I can't place it, though. It sounds familiar, but not really."

"Don't know, Jack. But if I had to lay money down, I'd say this guy knows more about you than we want him to."

Done talking, I leaned back in my seat and closed my eyes. The plane would land in thirty or forty minutes and that stretch of time might be my only shot at sleep for the next twenty-six hours.

I woke up after the plane had landed. First time I ever recalled sleeping through a landing. Sarah stood in the aisle, looking down at me, a smile across her face. For a moment, the situation facing us slipped my mind and I couldn't help but think about how beautiful she looked.

"What?" I said.

"You snore," she said.

"No," I said.

"Yes," she said.

"Prove it."

"How?"

"Bring a tape recorder to my house one night this week and sleep over."

She smiled, turned and walked to the open door at the front of the plane.

"Time to get serious, Jack," Frank said.

That was all it took. Everything that had happened in the past eleven hours rushed to the front of my brain, the weight of it nearly throwing me off balance. I glanced at my watch. Close to eleven a.m. I didn't let my mind do the calculations. Instead, I hopped in front of Frank and moved to the front of the jet, then down the small staircase that led to the ground. A black sedan waited for us. The driver's window rolled down and McKenzie nodded. I opened the door for Sarah and walked around the back of the car to get in on the other side. Frank sat up front.

"The office?" McKenzie asked.

"Hospital," Frank replied. "We need to go see Tammy Nockowitz."

We reached the hospital shortly after eleven a.m. I hesitated at the front door, waiting for my phone to ring. It didn't. But that didn't mean we weren't in for any surprises.

20

When we reached the room, it became obvious that Tammy wasn't in as good a shape as Harris had said. She faded in and out. Obvious head trauma, Sarah had informed us. Tammy smiled a little when she saw us surrounding her bed, and she fixed her eyes on me. I sat down on the edge, near her waist, facing her, like the night before.

"Tammy," I said. "We need for you to tell us everything that happened last night. What do you remember?"

She licked her lips and swallowed hard. Her words formed slowly. Her voice sounded raspy. "It's all bits and pieces. I remember being at the dinner, and then here. I also remember the accident."

"Let's start there, Tammy. What do you remember about the accident?"

"A man." She paused and blinked hard. "Several men."

"Paramedics?"

"No."

"Cops?"

"No."

"Firefighters?"

"No," she said forcefully. "I didn't see any flashing lights, like you'd see if the cops or medics were there. Only flashlights and men."

"What did they say?"

"I... I don't recall."

"How did they talk?"

"What do you mean?"

"Accents? Did any of them have a British accent?"

Frank flinched back and shot me a look. I shrugged in return. I figured that if she was forced to remember something we didn't think was a possibility, it might jog her brain enough to recall actual facts.

"No, I'd remember that," she said.

"Do you remember anything at all about them that might have been different?"

"They were Hispanic, or looked that way, at least."

"All of them?" I asked.

"All but one. One was white. American. I... I think I recognized him from somewhere."

"From where?"

Her eyes closed and her head fell back into the pillow and tilted to the side an inch. Out cold. We waited by her side. None of us spoke. We all stared at Tammy, waiting for her to come to. Finally, she did, and she picked right back up where she had left off.

"The party," she said.

"What about it?" I said.

"I saw the man there."

"Can you identify him?"

She looked around and then lifted a bruised arm and pointed at Frank. "Him."

Frank took a step back and shook his head. "What?"

"What about him?" I said.

"I remember him from the party," Tammy said.

"And then at the accident?"

"What accident?" Her face contorted. She shook her head, just once in each direction. Then she passed out, again.

I looked at Sarah and held out my hands in a *what-the-hell* gesture.

"She's got a nasty concussion," she said. "Head trauma. Never know how someone will react."

"This is getting nowhere," Frank said. "I was with you all night, Jack."

"I know, Frank. That's not a concern. We'll have to see what she says when she wakes up. Remember, first thing she said to me last night was, 'they got him.'"

We waited for Tammy to rejoin us. Seconds turned into minutes. Minutes passed in bunches. I looked at the clock on the wall and it was close to eleven-thirty a.m. Close to a day left, according to the man on the phone. I half-imagined that he'd turn out to be a prophet. The countdown he gave me would turn out to be a doomsday timer, and when the world didn't end, as per usual, he'd restart the timer. Maybe tell me I had two years, three months, and four days left.

"I'm going to grab some coffee," Frank said. "Anyone else want a cup?"

Sarah nodded and so did I.

"OK," Frank said. "Three coffees."

He slipped out of the room.

Sarah turned to me. "I thought our first date would be much more romantic than this."

I smiled at her, then glanced down at the broken woman who lay unconscious on the bed. The smile faded from my lips and I thought of another line of questioning that might be relevant.

Sensing my mood was too somber to discuss the start of our relationship, Sarah switched gears. "How did you manage to keep the cops out of this?"

I shrugged, unsure of how much I should tell her. "As you've seen by now, we have our own way of doing things."

"Yeah. And...?"

I eyed her for a moment, and then said, "Nobody messes with us. We've got the contacts to make things happen. Our boss's boss is a powerful man. The kind of man people avoid stepping on the toes of. If we want things to work a certain way, he goes to bat for us, and things work the way we want."

She crossed her arms over her chest and shook her head. "You're talking in circles."

"Possibly."

She huffed and I smiled.

A nurse stuck her head in the room and told us that she needed us to step out for a few. Sarah nodded, and since she was the resident expert in all things emergency medicine, I followed her out of the room. We headed toward the lobby, following signs that directed us to the cafeteria. Saw Frank a hundred yards down the hall and met him halfway.

He pulled Sarah's coffee out of a cardboard drink holder, then mine, and then he asked, "What's going on?"

"They had to run some tests," Sarah said.

Frank nodded at Sarah and then turned his head toward me. He reached out and gestured behind him. "There's an empty waiting room back there. Let's sit for a few and figure out the best way to go about questioning her."

21

THE ROOM WAS DIM AND THE AIR WAS STILL AND STERILE.
The smell of disinfectant was stronger here than in any other
area of the hospital. It had a single door for entering and exiting,
and it had been closed, providing no air exchange. Trapped
Lysol, or whatever the hell they used in a place like this,
prevailed. Sarah leaned against the wall next to a framed
painting I'd never seen before. The artist has splashed red and
purple and brown and yellow paint on the canvas. Randomly, I
assumed. However, the way the colors spread, dripped, mixed
and mingled formed an image. A tree and a sapling, or a flower
and a petal, or a mother and child. Could have been all three.
Could have been a football stadium, for all I knew.

"So look," Frank said. "We need to get to the point with
this woman."

"What do you think we've been trying to do?" I said.

"I know, but with this in and out." He paused to take a deep
breath, then exhaled loudly. "We need to figure out where her
mind is as soon as she's up."

I looked at my watch. Eleven forty-five. "What if she doesn't remember?"

Frank swiveled in his chair and nodded toward Sarah. "Is that possible?"

Sarah's head bobbed up and down. "Yeah, unfortunately. Not likely permanent. But quite possibly temporary."

"Shit," Frank said.

"Yeah," I said.

"So I guess we play it by ear, then," Frank said.

"So we're right back where we started," I said.

He nodded.

I stood up, stretched my back. Yawned and glanced at the TV. The images didn't register, at least not at that moment.

"Ready to go back?" Frank said.

"Yeah." I took a few steps toward the door and stopped when I noticed Sarah staring at the TV.

"Hey, hey," she said. "That guy looks familiar."

Frank turned and stared up at the images on the screen. "That's Senator Burnett. Hell, we were having drinks with him last night."

"Turn up the volume," I said.

Sarah stood on the tips of her toes and pressed the up volume button until we could hear the reporter. The news wasn't good. Burnett had gone missing. He didn't return home after an event last night, according to his wife.

Frank shook his head. "Next thing you know, we'll be getting a call to look for him."

"Guy's corrupt, from what I've heard," I said. "Maybe it caught up to him."

"He seemed all right to me," Sarah said.

"You're in the business of saving people," Frank said. "Everyone has to be OK to you, otherwise you'd have to let half of them die on principle." He walked to the door and looked over his shoulder, then said, "I don't like this, Jack. The mother hurt in what appears to be a malicious hit and run. Some creep calling you. Now a U.S. Senator is missing. And not any Senator, one with ties to us."

"Let's get back to the room," I said. "We need to get Harris to reach out to all teams and get a status update. We need to verify that everyone is accounted for and that no one else has been harmed."

We hustled down the hall, faster than a walk, slower than a run, not quite a jog, turning left into the corridor that led to Tammy's room. The latest revelation had me on edge. I knew Tammy's place in all of this. She'd had the misfortune of being the kid's mother. Whoever was behind this wanted to get the kid to get to me. I'd screwed up their little group, disrupted their game. Now they turned their bats toward me. But what did the Senator have to do with this? I couldn't make sense of it. I didn't know much about his policy or even what state he represented. I knew it was something I'd have to look into once we got back to headquarters.

I ran the last fifty feet to Tammy's room, extending my right arm to grab hold of the doorframe and stop myself. Tammy lay in her bed, unconscious, as expected. What I didn't expect was to see the man who stood next to her bed, needle in his hand, plunging it into her arm. He looked over his shoulder and smiled at me.

"Who the hell are you?" I said.

His smile broadened. "She'll be out for a while."

The man didn't look like a doctor or a nurse or someone who should be in the room. It wasn't his hair, or his clothes, or his face. It was his shoes. The dirty, scuffed combat boots he had on had no place in a hospital.

I drew my gun and aimed it at his head. Frank entered the room. The man turned and lifted his arms. The needle hung from Tammy's pale forearm. A thin line of blood seeped out, letting gravity determine its path.

"What's going on in here?" Frank said.

"He just injected her with something," I said.

The man slowly turned with his arms in the air. "Only to keep her quiet for a bit, that's all." He looked at me and I looked at the mirror. He turned his head, then said, "Silly me, I left it in her." He turned around and withdrew the needle from her arm. He didn't turn back around slowly, though. Instead he whipped around, pistol in his hand.

I pulled my trigger before he managed to square up. The bullet hit him in the side of the head. A cloud of blood hovered where he stood and coated the wall behind him.

Sarah took a step into the room and stopped. Her face skewed and shock filled her eyes. "What the hell happened?"

"We need to get her out of here," I said. "Now."

Sarah went to work, freeing the woman from the wires that bound her, and then freeing the bed. She started pushing it toward the door.

"Stop," I said.

"What?" she said.

"That won't work. What are we going to do? Steal an ambulance?"

"What do you suggest then?" she said.

"There." Frank stood outside the room and pointed at a wheelchair.

"That's crazy," Sarah said. "We don't know the extent of her injuries."

"We know she has a concussion and we'll have to assume that's it." I picked Tammy up and stepped into the hall. Frank arrived with the wheelchair two seconds later and helped me set her down. "Frank, go get the car. We'll meet you outside."

Two members of the hospital's security department were

running down the hall toward us. They shouted something, probably stop, but I didn't bother to listen. I started to push Tammy in the opposite direction. The only problem was that they were moving faster than I could with a wheelchair in front of me. I heard one of them yell *Jesus Christ*, and I assumed they'd reached the room and looked inside. The echo of their footsteps ceased, and without looking back, I figured they entered Tammy's room.

The emergency exit doors loomed in the distance. There was enough separation between the room and us that we had a good chance of making it. "Go open those doors, Sarah."

She ran ahead and hit the doors full speed, placing one hand on the red and silver handle and planted her shoulder into the middle of the door. It popped open, letting natural light flood of the hallway. A piercing alarm blared through the corridor. The squeal penetrated my ears and was certain to rouse at least one of the guards.

I slowed as I approached the open doorway. I could see that the concrete walkway stretched out about six feet, but it had no rail to stop us from going over the edge if I burst through too fast. I'd dump Tammy out of the wheelchair, sending her careening into the asphalt. I angled the wheelchair through and descended the ramp as quickly as possible with Sarah on my heels.

"Stop," the guard shouted from behind.

I pulled my sidearm and reached back and shot into the wall above his head. He ducked into the building as chunks of plaster rained down. He slammed the emergency exit door shut.

"What the hell are you doing?" Sarah rose from the squatting position she took when I reached around with the gun. Her hands were still on her head and fire was in her eyes.

"Swatting a fly." I pushed on, toward the end of the building. A car nosed around the corner. I quickly judged it as being a government vehicle. Only question I had was whether it was

Frank or the police. They gave us leeway, but I shot and killed a man inside the hospital. That would require significant ironing to straighten out, and would likely have to come from someone far above my pay grade.

The car pulled all the way around the corner and I recognized Frank in the driver's seat. He pulled up next to us and jumped out.

"Sarah," I said. "You get in the back with Tammy."

"OK."

She slid into the back seat. I lifted Tammy and sat her next to Sarah, who helped steady the woman. Ten seconds later, we were racing behind the hospital toward a rear exit, on our way back to headquarters.

22

I LEANED BACK IN MY CHAIR AND PLACED MY FEET ON MY desk, crossed at the ankle. The sound of the ringing cell phone was stifled inside my pocket. It was barely audible. I cursed myself for switching it off vibrate. The display read *Unknown caller*. The clock said twelve p.m.

"Twenty-four-"

"Yeah, I got it," I said. "You don't have to keep reminding me."

The man laughed. "So, Mr. Noble's got it, does he?"

"What do you want?"

The man said nothing.

"What happens in twenty-four hours?"

"Time runs out."

"For what?"

"You're about to find out."

"Who the hell are you?"

"You're about to find that out, too."

I stood and walked around my desk to the open doorway of my office. The lobby was deserted and silent. Frank stepped out of the infirmary, his mouth open, as if he was about to say something. I held a single finger in the air to stop him.

"Give my best to Ms. Nockowitz," the man said. "If she ever wakes up again, that is."

I flipped the phone shut without responding. Tossed it on my desk and left my office, slamming the door shut behind me. Frank waited in the center of the lobby, hands in his pockets. His shoulders were slightly hunched forward and his head down.

"What is it?" I said.

"She's up."

Good news for us, bad for the guy, I thought.

I stepped into the infirmary, nodded at Doc, and smiled at Tammy. She twisted the left side of her mouth into a smile and blinked slowly.

"She OK?" I asked.

Doc nodded and said, "We countered what they put in her. She's going to be fine."

"Can she handle questioning?"

"Yes. As long as it's not the way you normally do it."

"OK," I said. "Leave."

The doctor puffed his cheeks and then blew the air out in a burst, letting his lips flap together. Perhaps he wanted to argue with me and decided against it. I didn't watch him leave the infirmary, only heard the door close behind me, leaving Frank and me alone with Tammy.

"Tammy," I said. "I'm going to be asking you some hard questions. I need you to answer the best you can. OK?"

"OK," she said.

"Tell me about Christopher's father."

"There's nothing to tell."

"What do you mean?"

"He left a long time ago."

"Where did he go?"

"Go," she said with a chuckle. "That would imply he was there to begin with."

"So would saying he left."

She pursed her lips and nodded. "He's not in the picture. He's never been in the picture. Can we leave it at that?"

"When's the last time you had contact with him?"

She glanced between Frank and me and then let her eyes settle on the wall behind me. "Years ago. I asked him for help. Never heard back."

"Tammy?" I said.

"Yeah?" she said.

"Why are you lying to me?"

"I..." She looked away.

"We're trying to help. I think the boy's father has something to do with this."

I noticed Frank straighten and assumed he was a bit confused. This wasn't something we had talked about. In fact, I didn't know where I was going with the questioning. But limited time called for a change in procedure.

A tear gathered in the corner of her right eye. It built up until it could hide in the well no more. It slid down the side of her face and dripped onto her pillow, leaving a tiny stain that faded almost as soon as it appeared. "I want my son back, that's all. I didn't mean for this to happen."

"What do you mean you didn't mean for this to happen?" I said.

She sobbed lightly, but said nothing.

"Tammy?" I said, raising my voice.

She still said nothing.

"Dammit, Tammy, we're trying to help." My voice had escalated to a yell, and the door behind me burst open. "Get the hell out of here, Doc," I said.

"It's Sarah, and you need to take it easy on her."

"I know what I'm doing."

"Do you?" Sarah said.

She had a point. Did I? Lack of sleep and an overabundance of stress had me stretched to the max. I took it out on the poor woman who'd been beaten and battered and had her son taken from her. I decided to back it up and start over.

"OK, Tammy," I said. "Aside from me and Frank, did you recognize anyone at the dinner last night?"

She nodded.

"Who?"

"Vernon Burnett."

"From seeing him on TV?"

"No."

"Where?"

She said nothing. Tears filled her eyes and soon streamed down her cheeks. She sobbed lightly.

"Tammy?" I said. "Talk to me."

"You thought I was coming onto you, didn't you?"

This time I said nothing.

She forced a puff of air that I figured had been meant to sound like a laugh. "I guess I wanted you to think that. You seemed to like me. I mean, you smiled and looked at me."

Her words made little sense to me, almost like she'd begun babbling to throw me off the previous question.

"But," she said, "that wasn't what I was doing. And then when I gave you my number, I thought my look conveyed what I meant."

"I don't have a clue what you're talking about, Tammy," I said.

Her face turned red and she lifted her clenched fists in the air. Her lips peeled back, revealing teeth gritted tight together. A half-scream, half-growl escaped through narrow gaps where her teeth didn't line up correctly, top to bottom.

The three of us flinched in reaction to the sound the woman produced. Sarah moved toward the bed.

I reached for the door, and said, "I'll get the doctor."

"Wait," Frank said. "Just wait."

Tammy eased back into the pillow that supported her upper back and neck and head. Her face went slack for a moment, and then she began to cry. Her crying lasted thirty seconds, maybe more. She took a few deep, shaky breaths and wiped her eyes with the backs of her hands. A meek smile crossed her face and she apologized for her outburst.

"I know the Senator," she said. She took a deep breath. "He's my son's father."

I straightened up and sensed the others in the room do the same. "Tammy, Burnett was reported missing after he didn't show up for work this morning."

She began to cry again. In between sobs, she said, "Oh my God, he's got my son."

23

I LEFT THE ROOM AND WENT STRAIGHT TO MY OFFICE. I HAD a name. I had a face. I had to find the bastard and put an end to this. I placed my thumb on the fingerprint reader that controlled the locks on my desk. A click followed a beep. I slid the top-drawer open and grabbed my keys and wallet and an extra gun.

Someone cleared their throat from outside my office. I looked up and saw Frank standing there.

"What are you doing, Jack?"

"Going to get Burnett."

"You don't know where he is."

"Yeah, but our buddy Pablo downstairs might."

Frank cocked his head to the side and lifted an eyebrow half an inch. "He's gone, Jack."

"Where?"

"Someone else is working on him now. Trying to get information we couldn't."

Frustration and raged mixed like two foreign chemicals that reacted negatively with one another. I stood and kicked my desk, sending it sliding three feet, almost tipping over. My monitor fell off the edge of the desk and collided with the floor with a crash.

"Who the hell took him?" I said.

Frank shrugged. "The order came from above me, Jack."

"What does this guy want?" I said. "If what she said is true, and he's the father, then he has the kid. That means he's the one calling me. What's he want with me?"

Frank stepped into my office. He kicked the door closed, then leaned back against it. He said nothing for a long while, stood there, staring at me.

The adrenaline surge faded, and my head cleared. I tried to process the new information logically. There had to be a reason this guy had a hard-on for me.

"I'm going to find out who's heading up the Burnett disappearance," Frank said. "And I'll get Harris and McKenzie involved. If anything, they can provide us with information that the news can't."

"OK," I said.

"I want you to stay in here. Relax. Wait for that next phone call."

"OK."

Frank stepped into the lobby, and then turned abruptly. "And if he calls when I'm not around, don't say a word about what Tammy told us."

I nodded, but he'd already turned away. I reset my desk and sat down behind it. Leaned my head back and somehow managed to fall asleep. A short, shallow sleep that probably did more harm than good.

I woke to the sound of my phone chirping and buzzing. It danced across the laminate desktop. I didn't have to look at the display to know that it would read *unknown caller*. It felt strange to read the words, knowing with ninety percent certainty that the voice on the other end belonged to Burnett. I didn't have to look at the clock to know it was one p.m. Twenty-three hours to go. Till what? Only the unknown caller knew. But I was about to find out. I flipped the phone open and held it up to the side of my face.

"I needn't give you my ominous greeting this time, correct, Mr. Noble?"

I nodded, then felt a bit sheepish, realizing he couldn't see me. "No. That part of our relationship is down pat."

The man laughed for the first time since revealing his voice. It was deep and raspy, from too many years of drinking and smoking, I assumed. I knew the laugh. I'd spent half an hour, at least, with that laugh the night before, sitting at the bar and shooting the breeze. There was no doubt in my mind that the man on the phone was Senator Vernon Burnett.

He stopped laughing and sighed. I had nothing to say, so I waited for him to make the next move.

"The time is now, Jack."

"You're turning the clock ahead?"

He snorted. "No. The time for you to move is now, Jack."

"Move where?"

"I need you to head to Miami."

"What's in Miami?"

"Well..." The man paused a beat too long. "I need you to take care of something down there."

"I'm not going."

"Then the boy dies."

"You're not going to kill the boy."

"I'm not? You a prognosticator now? You want to give me the winning lottery numbers while you're at it?"

I said nothing.

"Jack, you want this kid's blood on your hands?"

I said nothing.

"Miami. Alone. Commercial flight, not one of yours. Leave

for the airport now, because I'm going to call you at six p.m. and you better be ready to move again."

I had no choice. The guy had me by the balls. And for the first time in fourteen hours, I was happy about it. He was going to put me in position to take him down. He'd make a mistake. They always did.

"OK," I said.

"You know what?" He said. "Bring the woman with you, the brown haired one, but no one else."

I lifted my head and looked into the lobby. Sarah sat across the way with her back to the wall opposite mine. She looked in the direction of my office, but not at me. I knew that I couldn't drag her down there with me. Not on a suicide mission.

"Just me," I said.

I heard the sound of plastic banging on wood as he set the phone down, then the man's muffled voice. "Come here," it sounded like he said. His words were followed by a smack, then a scream. A child yelled, "Let me go." I didn't recognize the voice. The pitch was different, higher maybe, and more melodic. The voice belonged to a girl, not Christopher. My stomach dropped as I realized we'd lost one.

"She's a cute one, Jack," he said. "You should see her. You can't imagine the kind of money she'd bring in."

I buried my rage. "OK," I said, maintaining a calm and controlled tone. "Me and the woman. We're heading to Dulles now and we'll be in Miami by six." I ended the call.

My rage resurfaced. I tipped my desk and let it crash to the floor.

Frank appeared outside my office and yanked the door open. "What happened?"

"Who do we know in Miami?"

A confused look crossed his face. "What? Where?"

"Miami," I said. "Bottom of Florida." I stepped through the doorway and pushed past him into the lobby.

Sarah looked up at me and forced a smile. "What's up?"

"You're coming to Miami with me."

"What?"

I'd heard *what* too many times by that point. "Listen, there's no time for questions. He's got two kids now. He wants me in Miami. He wants you to go with me."

"I can't leave and go to Miami," she said.

"You don't have a choice," I said, my words seething with anger, though not directed at her.

"Wait a minute," Frank said. "Two kids?"

"Yeah."

"Who?" He held out his hands. "We had everyone covered."

"A girl," I said. "I'd suggest you call around and see who doesn't answer. That'd be the place to start."

"Christ," Frank said. "What are we dealing with?"

I shook my head. "I'll figure that out on the flight. But for now, we've got to move." I grabbed Sarah's hand and pulled her across the lobby, toward the exit. I stopped and turned. "And Frank, I need a contact down there. I'm stepping off a plane completely unarmed in a place where I don't know a soul."

24

I BLINKED MY EYES OPEN AND STARED THROUGH THE OVAL window, ignoring the glare from the sun and the smudges left behind from a previous passenger. From six miles in the air, the ground looked like scenery surrounding a toy train set. There were tracts of land, each a different shade of green or brown. Tiny black and gray asphalt roads and green rivers looked like snakes slithering through the serene setting.

I glanced to my left and saw Sarah leaning back, passed out. We both needed some sleep, and I was glad to see she would get more than I had. My watch said it was four p.m., which meant we'd probably already crossed the Georgia-Florida border and had less than an hour until we landed in Miami.

Burnett had only given us five hours to make the trip. Hardly enough time to get to the airport, book the first available flight, make it through security and then hop on a two-and-a-half hour non-stop flight from D.C. to Miami. We'd made it, though, managing to sprint onto our two-thirty flight as they were closing the door. Of course, my false F.B.I. credentials helped convince the airline staff to let us on. If caught, I'd likely spend a day in a cell. No more than two. And I'd be waiting for one of four people to come and clear me. That's how clandestine we were.

I returned my gaze to the window and the clouds and sky and perfect landscape below, sectioned off into square and rectangular plots. People think of resorts, theme parks, and South Beach when they think of Florida. The strip of country, farm, and swampland that runs through the center corridor of the state was often forgotten, and certainly ignored, by vacationing families and escaping snowbirds.

The greenness of Florida was in stark contrast with the day old snow that covered D.C. and New Jersey. I shrugged off my coat, acknowledging for the first time I wouldn't need it in Miami, maybe not ever again, for that matter. Just as the snow would soon melt away and soak into the ground or evaporate into the sky, I'd soon be recycled and returned to the Earth. I couldn't think like that, though. I didn't have time to think like that. Two innocent lives were on the line. Three if I counted Sarah. Countless more if I didn't put a stop to Burnett.

I refocused and replayed the last week in my mind. The events of the past thirty hours were my primary focus. At this point, I figured there was a ninety-five percent chance Burnett would be the man I'd be face to face with in Miami. Facts were he'd gone missing, and if I was to believe Tammy, he'd fathered her child and then abandoned them. I figured out the motive there easily enough. He had his political career to think of, and I doubt he abandoned them entirely. Probably paid her off, either one time or continuing to this day. Maybe he got tired of it. Maybe that's why he had the boy taken. The men that were the guts of the operation wouldn't question an order handed down by him. Sure, most of the kids had been taken at random, but

Christopher had been targeted. I was sure of it. Pablo's statement of smacking the mother, and the bandage on Tammy's head confirmed it. Then the boy had been targeted a second time. He'd been pulled from the wreckage, supposedly. Something about the wreck bothered me. Tammy had been pretty banged up, and the car mangled. None of us were experts, although Sarah came close, but it sure looked like the only person who could have survived that crash would have been the driver. Of course, a little kid might not have been impacted. Without seeing the car in person, making that determination was damn near impossible.

Burnett had apparently masterminded the ring. Why, though? Why would a U.S. Senator get involved in such a thing? Money was the obvious answer, but there had to be more to it than that. Had he fallen in with the wrong people? Wrote checks his ass couldn't cash, as they say? Perhaps someone had information on him, damaging information. Perhaps the kind of thing that could ruin the man's career. In exchange for keeping quiet, he'd been recruited to oversee the group. He had power. He had connections. It still didn't make sense, to me, at least. On the other hand, having the boy kidnapped did, for any number of reasons.

I felt like a man running a marathon, only I was stuck at the two-mile mark. The answer was right in front of me, but I couldn't see it through the thousands in the crowd that swarmed by me while I took endless step after endless step on a treadmill.

Finally, what did Burnett want with the boy now? Bait? I figured that's why he had the girl. If not bait, then presumably to escape with him. I knew that escape had to be in the plans. He said to come alone, but he knew all about me, so he said to bring Sarah, too. I presumed as a bargaining chip. He also knew who I worked for. And he had to be prepared for them to show up at some point, which meant he did not intend to stay in Miami after he'd finished with me.

Sarah's arm brushed against mine. I turned toward her and saw her eyes flutter open. Warm, soft, inviting. She arched her back, dropped her head, moaned. The sound sent a shiver through me.

"Where are we?" she said.

"In between Orlando and Tampa."

"They're kind of across from each other, aren't they?"

I nodded then smiled. Anyone watching might assume we really were two lovers on vacation. Worst case, they'd think we were two colleagues on a business trip. Not a single person on the plane, not even Sarah, would guess that we were two people on a suicide mission. I was the only one with that distinction.

"Will we have time to find a hotel?" she asked with a single eyebrow raised curiously.

I shook my head. "Unfortunately, not with Miami traffic at five p.m. We'll have to wait for the next call at the airport and then figure out where to go."

Of course, I knew where we'd be going, and it wouldn't be to a hotel. I didn't tell her that, though.

"Do you think Frank will come through with a contact to meet us and...?"

I nodded. A gesture betrayed my feelings. Frank would come through, that much was true. But we'd never meet the man. I knew that.

"We'll have to play it by ear," I said. "If at any time you feel uncomfortable, I want you to tell me. And I want you to go. Leave."

She shook her head and placed her hand on mine. "I'm not going anywhere, Jack."

I smiled while my stomach knotted. I trusted myself to get

through this OK. But could I trust myself to get her through it too? Bravery was second nature for her. I wasn't sure if her instincts were right for this job.

She closed her eyes again, and so did I. Neither of us spoke again until the plane landed.

25

THE AIRPORT HUMMED WITH ACTIVITY. PEOPLE COMING and going, and waiting for loved ones with anticipation, and watching them leave with sorrowful eyes. For me, it was another day at work. For Sarah, it was like a shot of adrenaline. I bet if I'd asked, I'd have found out the woman liked to jump out of planes and off bridges and go to one of those places where they let you drive a real race car around a real race track. The thought excited me, and for a second, I let my mind wander to what we'd do together if we survived this situation.

We picked our way through the crowd that surrounded the arrival's gate. Parts of it felt like scraping through molasses. For some, courtesy had been checked at the door that day. Sarah stayed close as we passed through the thickest spots. Her chest pressed against my side, arm wrapped around my waist. I found myself wishing we were two lovers on vacation. I'd have settled for colleagues on a business trip, that is if she insisted on remaining that close.

The crowd thinned and Sarah pulled away. Not much, only

an inch or two. Her arm slid off my waist and wrapped around my arm. It felt comfortable and natural. Too much so, though. I found myself thinking more of her than paying attention to the crowd and the people that waited by the exit doors fifty yards ahead. Letting them spot us first was a recipe for disaster and something I generally tried to avoid.

Fortunately, I spotted him before he spotted me. He looked to be my height. His body was thin and athletic looking. He wore a dark blue suit with a conservative tie. His brown hair was cropped close to his head, with sunglasses perched atop. Knock ten years off Frank and he and the man would be spitting images of each other.

I exhaled a heavy sigh of relief. It didn't go unnoticed by Sarah.

"What is it?" she asked.

"Frank came through for us," I replied.

"Who? Where?"

"By the front door. Blue suit. Boring tie. Frank minus ten years."

Her head turned left, then right, then stopped. "I see him." A smile crossed her face. Mine, too. We'd be safe, for a while.

We walked another twenty-five yards. I deliberately slowed our pace down. I wanted him to see us. I had to see his reaction. Not that I didn't trust Frank to come through for us. That wasn't it at all. I was overly cautious when it came to meeting new people. And his initial reaction would tell me everything I needed to know.

The man's head inched side to side. He let his eyes do to the bulk of the work. They scanned left to right, corner to corner. No face went unnoticed. Finally, his gaze landed on me. It was judgment time. His lips parted and turned up in a smile. He mouthed, "Jack," and waved both hands above his head.

I kept moving forward, same pace. I looked to his left and to his right. I checked beside me, then beside Sarah. Everything felt normal. Frank had come through for us. I almost felt bad for doubting him, then I realized he would have doubted me if the tables were turned.

I lifted my right hand above my head and waved. I nodded, smiled, and kept moving. Fifteen yards away. His smile broadened. Ten yards away. His smile faded. Two more steps. He looked left, then right. A new grin swept across his face, but his eyes were narrow, beady, and dark. I felt a hand on my elbow. I felt Sarah pulled away from me. She gasped, and then went quiet, presumably because she felt the barrel of a gun pressed into her side, poised to rip through her kidney. I knew she felt that because I felt the same thing.

Frank hadn't come through, not by a long shot. This guy was one of Burnett's men.

26

The men led us through the steel-rimmed glass exit doors. The hot, muggy Miami air hit me like a sledgehammer. I started sweating within sixty seconds. We crossed the street like a misfit rat pack.

The man in the suit stopped in front of a white Cadillac Escalade. The vehicle was adorned with gold trim. They shoved Sarah and me in the back row. The men that guided each of us with guns in our backs, respectively, sat in the middle row Captain's chairs. They twisted in their seats to keep weapons trained on me. They didn't view Sarah as a threat. I didn't blame them. She was too easy on the eyes to be a threat. Of course, that could make her more of one. However, Burnett knew who he was dealing with. He had access to my files, classified or not.

The man in the suit climbed into the passenger seat and nodded at the driver, who adjusted the mirror. The driver's head twisted and turned up. His eyes burned into me. Those eyes, dark and puffy, looked familiar. He twisted at the waist, stuck out his left arm and grabbed a hold of the seat next to him, then turned his head.

"*Hola*, Jack."

It took a fraction of a second for me to recognize the man. *Pablo*. The guy who had led us to the house. The guy who'd been beaten within an inch of his life by Frank. The guy who'd supposedly had a heart attack at SIS headquarters. Now, the guy who surely wanted to have the first crack at me.

I nodded without breaking eye contact. Pablo was scared of me before, and I'd do everything to maintain that power over him, no matter my personal predicament.

"Let's go, Pablo," the man in the suit said, dragging out the o in Pablo's name two beats too long. "Too many damn cops around here."

The men in the car laughed. Inside joke, I figured.

Pablo looked away and fired up the engine. Put the SUV in reverse and pulled out of the parking lot. Every time he looked into the rear view mirror, his eyes shifted between my eyes and the road behind me. I grinned, a little. He narrowed his eyes, a lot.

Sarah nudged me with her knee. I turned my head and saw pleading in her eyes. *Do something*, she mouthed. She might as well have said it, as I was sure when I looked, the guys in the middle row did so as well.

"Any chance we can stop at a diner for something to eat?" I said.

"Shut up, Noble," the man in the suit said.

"How about a drive-thru then?"

"How about you shut up before I have one of them feed the girl a lead lunch?"

I turned to Sarah, shrugged, and mouthed the word *sorry*. She rolled her eyes, shook her head. I reached out and grabbed her hand.

"None of that, man," the guy sitting in front of her said.

She tried to pull away. I wouldn't let go.

The guy in front of her lifted his arm and aimed the gun at her forehead, leaving about four inches between barrel and flesh. It'd be impossible to miss at that distance.

"Let go," he said.

"Do it," I said. "Go ahead. You're going to do it later, anyway. Get it over with now."

I saw the light glint off the barrel of the gun a half second before the man in front of me slammed it into my forehead. My head snapped back like it was attached to a swivel on my neck. It rebounded forward violently. Warm blood flooded over my brow, into and around my eye, and down my cheek. It dripped onto my shirt and pants.

"Jack!" Sarah said.

I held my left arm out, across her chest like we had hit the brakes and were skidding and I wanted to prevent her from flying through the window.

"It's OK," I said. "Only a cut."

It wasn't OK. The head wound I suffered the week before made any blow to the head that much more severe. I knew that. She knew that. But I couldn't let these men know that.

One of them threw me a towel. I figured it was dirty, but couldn't tell. One eye was flooded with blood, the other with salty tears. It was like I was underwater and nothing looked clear. Sarah grabbed the towel from my hand and wrapped it around my head, cinching it tight so it slowed down the flow of the blood through the wound.

"Gonna shut up now, Jack?" the man in the suit said.

I said nothing. Stared straight ahead and settled in for the ride. I tried to pay attention to the streets we followed, but everything passed in a blur. Had my brain begun to swell? Or was it the effects of sleep deprivation? How long had it been since I had more than a few hours of sleep? Two days or three? I couldn't remember. Wasn't sure what day it was anymore.

The localized ache at the site of the wound expanded, at first across my forehead. Then it wrapped around both sides, and then toward the middle. My brain hurt and felt like it had split into two. I saw stars in front of me, literally. I never believed anyone when they said that, but at that moment, I knew it to be true. The stars faded away into pinpricks of light punched into fabric.

Sarah whispered my name, perhaps sensing or more likely realizing that something was wrong.

I responded in kind, I think. I felt the hum of her name in my throat but couldn't tell if my lips parted.

"Jack!" Sarah's voice was loud, but muffled, like we were under water. The pleasant tone of her voice replaced by a thundering clap containing four letters, J-A-C-K.

"What the hell is going on back there?" A man's voice. The man in the suit, I assumed, only because there was no accent. It sounded garbled, not like it was underwater, but speaking through a mouthful of water.

The sensation of fire spread through my head, while ice filled my veins and froze my body in place. I tried moving my arms and couldn't. Tried to kick with my legs, but they remained rooted to the floor.

Delicate hands grabbed my arms. Sarah, I figured, although I couldn't see to verify it was her touch. I felt the weight of her body over mine.

"We need..." Her voice faded into the depths. "...hospital..." Gone again.

Then the sensation in my hands and feet and legs and arms disappeared. A black curtain hung before my eyes. The pain in my head retreated. I thought that perhaps I'd died.

27

I HADN'T DIED. IT DIDN'T TAKE ME LONG TO COME TO THIS conclusion, although I did determine it while still passed out. Wherever I was at that moment, the place stood empty. Silent. When my time came, there'd be the souls of all those who'd perished at my hand. They'd be standing around waiting for me in an effort to be the one to capture my soul. Of all things in life, I was sure of that.

Slowly, the sensation returned to my hands, feet, legs, and arms. The pain started in the center of my brain and expanded outward, swelling and encompassing my head, and then retreating toward the spot of the gash on my forehead. The black curtain covering my eyes lifted. I stared ahead, unfocused, through a watery veil.

A thunderclap exploded to my left. "Jack!"

I blinked hard and looked to the right, out the window. The Escalade had stopped and high hedges, dark green through the tinted window, blocked any further view.

"Jack," Sarah said. "Can you hear me?"

I shifted my eyes to the left and turned my head until I saw her, then said, "Yeah."

She wrapped her arms around my neck. I felt her cheek against mine, her breath, hot and rapid, floating across my lips. I looked straight ahead and saw all four men staring at me, their brows furrowed, expressions of horror and confusion on their faces.

"What?" I said.

"Pull through, Pablo," the man in the suit said, turning in his seat to face forward once again. He took a final look at me and shook his head.

"You sure you're OK?" Sarah said.

"Yeah, I think," I said. "What the hell happened?"

She touched my forehead with a gentle hand, wiping blood from my brow. "You started convulsing, shaking. I thought you'd had an aneurysm and were dying on me."

I forced a smile. "I'm not going anywhere."

"Good. Don't."

I strained to look past Pablo and the man in the suit. A black iron gate with twists and curls at the top and the bottom opened up and we pulled through. The artificial light faded and it was hard to make out the landscape beyond the edges of the drive-way. I glanced down at my watch. Seven p.m. I looked back up. The house stood off in the distance another hundred yards or so. Pools of light adorned the facade, cast from garden lights spaced precisely across the front of the house. The calming pinkish orange hue of the stucco instilled a sense of relaxation in me. I knew it wouldn't last long, though. This was the last stop before whatever was to come next. And I was certain that the next stop wouldn't be any more pleasant than the seizure I'd experienced.

Pablo pulled up to the three-car garage and idled while a wide white garage door lifted open. Then he pulled the vehicle in and stopped. He stepped out. The man in the blue suit remained and turned to face us. Pulled out his sidearm and aimed it in my direction. The men in the middle seats got out on their sides of the car, respectively, then Sarah, and finally me and the man in the suit at the same time.

Pablo led the way into the house. We walked through a mudroom connected to the laundry room, then down a short hall, maybe ten feet long. It deposited us into the kitchen.

A man stood in front of an open refrigerator. He had on khaki cargo shorts and a blue t-shirt. He looked over his shoulder, revealing half his face. He recognized me instantly, as I did him. Senator Vernon Burnett.

"Hello, Jack," he said. "And this lovely lady is...?"

"Sarah," she said.

Burnett crossed the floor and stopped six feet away. "I might bring you with me, young lady." He smiled at her. His eyes traveled to me. The smile broadened. "Not you, though, Jack. I'm about through with you."

"Then get it over with," I said. "Shoot me now."

Burnett's smile faded a little. The corners of his mouth withdrew, but he kept his lips parted. His eyes narrowed, nostrils flared. Something about it got to him, so I figured best thing to do was keep at it.

"You don't have the guts," I said. "Do you?"

He chuckled and looked me up and down. "I don't have to, Jack. Any of these guys'll do it." He tossed a hand up with his thumb extended and pointed behind himself. "Especially Pablo. Man, was he pissed when he got down here."

"You got him out," I said, referring to Pablo while keeping my stare fixed on Burnett. No one had wanted to question him, I realized. It had been someone who worked for someone who worked for Burnett. They fed us that line and we bought it hook, line and sinker. The thought crossed my mind that maybe someone else high up in the government worked with Burnett on this.

He nodded. "When you've got the power and connections I've got, it's easy to make things like that happen."

"Who're the other guys?" I said.

Burnett took a deep breath and eyed me for a few seconds, then said, "They work for me. That's all you need to know."

"What about him?" I gestured with my head toward the man in the blue suit. "He doesn't seem like the others."

"You gotta have someone to watch the hens," Burnett said. "Reece is his name. He's a," he paused a beat and squished his lips to the side, like he was biting the inside of his cheek. "He's in some kind of law enforcement. We'll leave it at that."

"Corrupt," I said, looking Reece in the eye.

He smiled back at me. "The things we'll do for money, eh?"

"Yeah," I said, focusing on Burnett. "Why the kids, Senator? For the money?"

He took a deep breath, held it a moment, then exhaled loud enough for the sound to echo in the hallway behind me. "Frankly, Jack, that's none of your concern."

"Sick bastard," I said.

He cocked back and swung at me. I could have ducked or moved to the side and avoided it. Could have stepped inside and wrapped my arm around his, snapping the bones in his forearm or dislocating his shoulder or elbow. But I didn't. I let his fist connect with my jaw. The impact stung and sent me reeling back into the wall. I slid to the floor. He stood over me, eyes wild and dancing with adrenaline. Any trace of fear the man had of me disappeared at that moment. And that's exactly what I wanted to happen.

Two men from the SUV picked me up and dragged me through the house. We stopped in the middle of a hall. They pushed me up against a wall. One of them kicked my legs out to the side and pinned me there, my arm held high behind my back and his knee in my lower back. I watched the other pull out a key ring with at least two dozen copper keys. He shuffled through them and then inserted one into the door handle. It unlocked with a click. He wrapped his meaty hand around the knob and pushed the door open.

"Your new room," the man behind me said, only an inch or two away from my ear. His breath was hot against the side of my head and smelled like rancid fish.

"Alright, but don't get any ideas," I said. "I'm not in the mood for a threesome."

He grabbed me by my hair, pulled my head back and then slammed it forward. The impact left a dent in the drywall and hurt like hell. He'd managed to plant the majority of the impact on the same spot where he pistol-whipped me earlier in the car. I slid down the wall on the left side of my face, using my shoulder to keep me from crashing.

Two sets of hands picked me up. They pushed and pulled me, then tossed me into the room. They didn't close the door, though. The thin guy stood inside the room. The heavier guy stood behind him.

"He down?" Burnett said from the hall.

"He's ready for you," the skinny guy said as he stepped into the room with the heavier man a step behind.

Burnett followed them in and walked right up to me. "Easy or hard?"

I managed to get to my knees. Leaned my head back and looked him in the eye. Said, "Screw you."

Burnett shrugged and made an *I-don't-give-a-shit* face. Then he kicked me in the stomach with his right foot.

I bent forward, but refused to allow myself to collapse.

"Easy or hard?" he said again.

I couldn't speak, so I made a weak attempt to spit at him.

Saliva dove from my mouth, landing somewhere between us. A few drops of spittle landed on his shoes. Most of it hung from my lip in strands and fell from my chin and onto my chest.

"Don't be stupid, Jack." Burnett stepped back a few feet and took his eyes off me, which was the only thing that made me feel like they were through beating me up. "Pick him up and tie him to the bed."

The men wrapped their hands around my arms, dragged me across the floor to the bed. I ignored them and watched Burnett leave the room. He looked over his shoulder and made eye contact with me from the doorway. He shook his head, then disappeared down the hall.

The men tossed me onto the bed and right away, I felt heavy straps wrapped around my wrists. They cinched them tight, then did the same thing to my ankles. Finally, they drew a thick leather belt across my midsection and pulled it tight enough to draw me down into the bed. They cut the lights and left the room, leaving me to wonder what the hell was happening to Sarah at that moment.

My head and stomach ached from the beating I'd taken. I tried to pass out, but couldn't.

A streetlamp cast long fingers of light into the room. They stretched across my chest and legs, across the bed, and climbed up the walls. I counted the seconds to keep track of time. Got bored after thirty minutes and closed my eyes. Somehow, I managed to fall asleep.

I didn't wake until I felt a hand on my face, his hand. Burnett smiled when I opened my eyes.

"Hello, Jackie," he said.

I didn't greet him back.

"Twelve hours," he said.

That answered the question of how long I'd been asleep. It

was midnight and I'd been strapped to the bed for over four hours.

"You excited?"

I tried to shrug, couldn't.

"Where's Sarah?" I said.

He smiled then licked his lips. "She's fine. Cooperative, that one." He paused a beat and arched his eyebrows. "If you know what I mean."

I clenched my fists and tried to draw my arms upward, and was even less successful than I'd been at shrugging.

The smile faded from Burnett's lips and he leaned back, feigning a hurt look. "You've got to get past this, Jack. You and I, we should be friends. When it comes down to it, there's little difference between us."

I turned my head toward the window and said nothing.

Burnett stood and grabbed something off the nightstand. Upon closer inspection, it turned out to be a needle filled with clear liquid. He bent over me and slowly lowered the needle toward my forearm.

"What the hell is that?" I said.

He said nothing.

"Burnett," I said. "What the hell are you doing?"

He plunged the needle into my arm, striking a vein and releasing the venom into my bloodstream. A burning sensation worked its way up my arm and through my chest. Spread to my neck, then my head.

He turned his head to look at me, and said, "This is going to ensure that you sleep all night, Jack. And then tomorrow, it's going to make you cooperative."

I felt my senses dull, but managed to reply. "What's tomorrow?"

He pushed himself back up and walked to the door, then

turned around to face me once again. "You'll find out in twelve hours, give or take."

I didn't know if he cut the lights off or if the curtain in my head had been pulled over my eyes again, but the room went pitch black.

28

THEY STUCK SARAH AND ME ON THE REAR BENCH SEAT OF the Escalade again. The same two men sat in the middle seat, the skinny guy in front of me, the heavier guy in front of Sarah. I figured they did that so the big guy could come at me with momentum behind him if I gave him enough reason to do so. If he'd been placed in front of me, he'd have to loop around, giving me the advantage. Of course, it wouldn't matter now, not with handcuffs restraining me.

"Let's go," Reece said to Pablo, who once again sat in the driver's seat.

Burnett and another man were in the car in front of us. I could see the tops of three small heads bouncing as the car made its way down the driveway. I assumed the heads belonged to Christopher and the little girl. And another child I wasn't aware of.

For twenty minutes we drove. I wasn't familiar with Miami or its surrounding areas, having only passed through a couple times over the course of my life. But I was certain that the areas we drove through weren't popular tourist attractions. Old worn down buildings lined the streets. A mix of people filled the sidewalks, white, black and brown. They all looked poor, even the ones dealing drugs, a remarkable sight to kick off my final three hours.

It was nine a.m. and I had convinced myself that by five after twelve, I'd be dead. Sarah, too, I assumed, in some sense of the word. She'd either be lying next to me with no pulse or breath, or lying next to Burnett, her soul ripped from her body. I wondered if he'd kill one of the kids, perhaps two, leaving only his son alive. The only question I had was how many of the men I could take down with me. There were six of them. I'd already beaten Pablo mentally. The skinny guy wouldn't pose a problem, nor would the heavy one. I only saw the man riding with Burnett from the back and for a few seconds. Not enough for me to judge. Burnett didn't scare me. Reece concerned me. He had some sort of law enforcement or military training, which meant he knew how and where to hit. He also had size and strength on his side.

We turned off a four-lane road into an industrial complex. Corrugated steel warehouses lined the road as far as I could see.

I turned to Sarah and spoke for the first time since midnight.

"Are you OK?" I said, feeling stupid that of everything I could say that was what I chose.

She nodded.

"They didn't hurt you last night did they?" I asked.

She shook her head, but her face betrayed her. Her bottom lip quivered, slightly, only for a second. Her eyes glossed over. She blinked and looked away. I knew at that moment that they'd gotten to her last night. One way or another, they broke her spirit. I hoped that they hadn't damaged her physically.

"What happened?" I said it too loud.

"Shut up," Reece said. "Or I'll have them shut you up."

The heavy guy grinned and lifted his eyebrows a couple

times, taking too much pleasure in the thought of attacking a man restrained by handcuffs.

I brushed my left leg into Sarah's. She looked at me again, forcing a smile. I nodded in return, hoping she could read my mind. Because if she could, she'd know that I had plans to make sure every one of these men paid for what they'd done to her. They'd pay with their lives, but not before suffering by my hand.

I felt my body pull to the left and nearly toppled into Sarah. The car turned between two buildings, then turned again. We were now behind the last row of warehouses, a stretch of buildings that buffered the decrepit part of the city from the warm waters of the Atlantic. How many kids in those neighborhoods felt they had nowhere to go and saw these waters as a barrier, white capped waves pounding at them, keeping them away from a better life? The undertow existed solely to sweep away their dreams.

We rolled to a stop. I glanced between the four men in front of me and saw Burnett's car stop as well. Beyond his car was a large white semi-truck with no cargo container or trailer attached. Burnett stepped out of the car and walked to the semi. He reached into his pocket and fished around for a moment. Pulled his hand back out and dangled a key, which he inserted into the truck's driver side door. The door opened and he climbed into the cab. A minute later his feet emerged and he hopped down onto the pavement. He appeared to be empty handed, but I knew he hadn't gone in there for no reason. He turned toward our vehicle, smiled, and gave Reece a thumbs up.

Reece pulled out his cell phone and dialed a number. He placed the phone next to his head and waited. His eyes shifted and focused on the heavy guy, and I figured someone had answered the phone. "Bring it around," was all he said. Then he tucked the phone back into his pocket and opened his door.

Burnett met Reece halfway and the men spoke. Burnett was

animated while he talked. Reece used his hands to shield his eyes from the sun. What kind of person in law enforcement heads out without sunglasses? After a few minutes, Reece returned to the Escalade.

"Everyone out," he said.

Sarah stepped between the two men in front of us. The heavy one made her step over his lap to get out. He smiled. She didn't.

I bit back the rage that started to build inside. I had to save it for the right moment, which was sure to come soon.

Both men reached for me and pulled me out of the seat. They pulled me forward, and then pushed me through the open doorway. I managed to twist my body on the way to the ground and landed hard on my side. Better than landing on my face, I figured. Fire spread through my right hip, and I worried for a second it had been broken. As quickly as I'd hit the ground, they pulled me back to my feet and forced me to walk. My hip wasn't broken, but it hurt like hell.

Reece took over at that point. He wrapped one hand around my elbow, while the other held a gun that was loosely aimed at my stomach. He led me over to where Burnett stood.

"Jack," Burnett said. "Glad you are here to see this."

I said nothing.

Burnett arched an eyebrow and nodded toward Reece. Reece let go of me and started walking toward the roll up door cut into the building. He pulled a set of keys from his pocket. He knelt in front of the door and inserted the key into a padlock. It unlocked with a loud click. He stuffed the lock into his pocket, then lifted the door up and over his head, his arms stretching as high as they could and then pushing one last time to send the door atop the railing.

Burnett nudged me in the side. "What do you think?"

I scanned the forty-by-forty space and shrugged at the sight of dozens of boxes.

"Uncuff him, Reece," Burnett said. "He's going to do all the heavy lifting."

I turned my head to the left, then the right, trying to figure out where he wanted the stuff moved. The semi had no container, and there was far more here than could fit in the trunks of the vehicles we came in. Unless they were planning multiple trips, that is. I quickly shook that thought from my mind. They weren't going to drive this stuff away. Burnett was a missing man. The last thing he needed was to be found carting around all these boxes, not to mention his son, who was also missing.

An engine approached from behind. Its deep roar was easily distinguishable as not made by a car.

"That's my getaway car," Burnett said with a chuckle.

I waited a beat, then looked over my shoulder and saw the boat pull up and two men jump onto the pavement. They began to moor it to weathered and splintered wooden posts. The water must have been deep at that spot, because the boat was big, at least fifty feet long. It was the perfect getaway car. A half hour or so and you'd be in international waters. Freedom, in more ways than one.

"Pablo," Burnett said. "Take the woman and put her in the car with the kids. Take them around the other side."

"What're you doing with them?" I said.

"Insurance, Jack," Burnett said. "You do what I say and they'll be all right."

Something about his smile told me he was lying. But I wasn't ready to test him. Not yet.

The sedan pulled away. I was left standing with Burnett, Reece and the heavy guy.

"Start moving the boxes, Jack," Burnett said.

I wondered what the boxes contained. No point in asking Burnett, he'd never tell me. The bad guys only do that in the movies. I jammed my finger into the tape that sealed the flaps of the first box I came to. I wedged my fingers into the tiny slit and pulled back. The tape ripped off and one of the flaps lifted and fell to the side. Inside the box, I saw wads of cash, sealed in plastic wrap.

"Money?" I said.

"In that box," he said. He pointed at random and added, "Drugs in some of the others. Gold in a couple. Been amassing this stuff for a while, you see. I knew there might come a time I'd have to bolt. You know if things, uh, caught up to me, so to speak."

"You sold kids," I said. "Stole them from their parents and shipped them overseas."

"Not all of them," he said. "Hell, some of them are in better situations than they were in before."

"That's bullshit and you know it."

He made no attempt at rebuffing me.

"How's a man like you get involved in this?" I said.

"Money. Power."

"You have those things."

"They promised me more."

"Who's they?"

He laughed. "Agent till the end, eh, Jack?"

"And according to you, my end is near. Why not tell me who's behind this?"

"I'm not going to do that, Jack."

"We're going to get them. Frank will keep working this until the whole thing collapses, bringing you down with it."

"You're never going to shut this down. It's bigger than you, Frank, or the SIS. Ya'll might make some strides over here with the FBI, and overseas with the CIA, but I can assure you, I've got men in both agencies that will squash it. That's why no one ever got anywhere near close to us until you stuck your damn head in the way."

"It won't go away, Senator," I said. "Like Pandora's box. Once it's open, there's no going back."

Burnett got to his feet and walked in a semicircle in front of me. Back and forth, he went for a minute without saying anything. Then he stopped and looked past me, toward the boat or perhaps beyond, to a spot somewhere over the Atlantic.

"I'm coming back, Jack. Eventually my boy is going to come around and accept me as his father. Once he does, well, then it's a matter of time until he'll say whatever I tell him to say." He smiled and his eyes lit up. "Then it's a matter of getting back into the country. An anonymous tip will do the trick. Someone will send a group of Special Forces to rescue us. By the time they reach us, I'll have vanquished our captors. I come back to the U.S. a hero and adopt the boy I grew close to while held captive. He'll call me dad, and he'll mean it. But no one will know the truth but us. Should be enough to draw the majority vote."

I shook my head. "You're doing all this for political gain?"

His smile faded and he narrowed his eyes. His expression became quite serious.

"I'm doing all this to make my country a better place," he said.

I stood up and kicked the box to the side, then took two steps forward. We were only a foot or so apart. The smug look on his face faded, and I noticed his arms and shoulders grow tense.

"If that's what it's coming to, kill me now," I said.

He laughed, slow at first, then it built up. "Your time is coming, Jack. First you need to load my boat or the woman and the kids die."

I felt a hand on my back. It slid along my shoulder until it reached my collar, at which point I felt my body pulled backward, away from Burnett.

There were more boxes than I had anticipated. The room opened up to a second room, which contained roughly half the amount of cargo. For two hours, I made the trip from the warehouse, across the pavement, and onto the boat, where I loaded the cargo below deck. Reece kept a gun on me while I was in the warehouse and on the pavement. The men in the boat kept their guns on me, taking turns going below with me while the other stood at the top of the stairs. The process repeated itself over and over.

It was only a matter of time. Someone would get tired, look away and make a bad move. I was sure of it.

29

A HALF DOZEN BOXES REMAINED IN THE SECOND ROOM. They were bigger than the others, probably six feet long and three feet high and wide. I bent over the first and wrapped my hands around it until the tips of my fingers scraped the concrete floor. I slid them under the box and started to pull. Damn thing had to be a hundred and fifty pounds. It crossed my mind that there might be a human body in the box. Sweat dripped down my face and slid off my nose and chin and jawline, splattering on the box and proceeding to roll down to the floor.

I heard footsteps from outside the room. Two sets approached at a steady pace. Perhaps time was up.

"You can stop there, Noble," Burnett said.

I dropped the box, stood up straight, wiped the sweat from my brow. I tried to dry my hand on my shirt, but it was soaked. The south Florida humidity was a bitch if you didn't have a cold beer on hand.

"Turn around, Jack," Burnett said.

I scanned the room, looking for a weapon. I'd have settled for a baton right then. But the room was empty, except for the six boxes. And then I saw something that disturbed me. One of the boxes wasn't taped shut. The ends had been folded over one another to keep it shut. The dimensions matched the others in the room. All of them were large enough to fit me, slightly cramped since I had two inches on their length.

"C'mon," Burnett said. "Arms out and turn."

Dying in the back of a warehouse located next to a Miami ghetto held very little appeal to me. But if it was going to happen, I'd prefer to see the bullet coming. Go down with a fight. I lifted my arms out to the side, stopping halfway. I turned, slowly. I kept my head low, eyes up. I offered up as menacing a look as I could manage under the circumstances.

Burnett and Reece stood outside the doorway. Burnett aimed a pistol at me. Reece held a rifle at his waist, loosely aimed in my direction. He stepped back and Burnett motioned with his pistol for me to exit the room.

I stepped through the doorway and caught Burnett's eye on the way through. "What's in those boxes?" I asked, concerned that he intended to use one as my casket.

Burnett shrugged. "Let's go outside." He looked past me and added, "Reece, I want you to take him down there with the others."

I figured that the unsecured box wasn't meant for me. At least, not yet. I walked across the empty warehouse. Burnett followed. Reece stayed in front of me, walking backward, keeping a good ten feet between him and me. My foot hit the pavement. He pointed his gun at the Escalade, then back at me.

"Get in the back," Reece said.

I reached out and grabbed the door handle. It pushed open before I pulled. One of the men from the boat was inside. He held a pistol in his right hand.

"Don't try anything," the man said. "I'll shoot if you so much as sneeze."

I did my best to look unimpressed while I pulled myself up and into the car. I took a seat and waited. A few minutes later Reece opened the driver's door and hopped in behind the wheel. He fired up the V-8 engine and dropped the transmission into drive. We inched around the semi, then slowly drove on the pavement in between a long warehouse and the ocean. He stopped where the building ended.

"Get out," he said. Then he turned to look at the man sitting next to me. "Take him to the others and walk back."

"You're not waiting?" the man said.

"Would I tell you to walk back if I was?"

The man shook his head and held out his arms. He stared me down for a couple of seconds, and then said, "Let's go, man."

"This isn't over, Reece," I said.

He smiled and leaned toward me. "Yes, it is." He started to turn in his seat, then stopped. "Oh yea, Burnett had a message he wanted me to relay to you."

"What's that?"

"Time's up."

I glanced at my watch and saw it was ten till noon.

I opened the door. The sound of waves lapping against the concrete barrier greeted me. They carried a rhythm all their own. The man's feet hit the ground and his hand hit my back. He pushed me toward the end of the building. When we reached it, he said, "Turn left."

I did and saw Pablo, the heavy guy and the skinny guy, as well as Sarah. She stood with her back to a car. Her wrists were bound together by rope. The closer I got, the more obvious it became that she'd been crying.

"Sarah," I said.

She looked in my direction. At first her face scrunched up, as if she were about to start sobbing. She filled her lungs with salt air and exhaled, seemingly to steady herself.

I got within six feet of her and Pablo told me to stop. From that distance, I could see inside the car. The two kids sat in the back seat. Neither of them were Christopher. Were their hands bound, too? I couldn't tell.

"Arms behind your back," Pablo said.

I didn't move.

"Don't make this any more difficult than it has to be," he said.

I still didn't move.

Pablo did. He punched me in the kidney with his left hand and then reached for my arm. "How's that feel, huh?"

I said nothing. My body bowed sideways to the right. Pain spread from the point of impact to the middle of my abdomen. He had my left arm pinned behind my back with his plaster cast and managed to get my right halfway around.

"Someone help," he said.

The heavy guy jogged forward and planted a knee in my midsection. I was surprised that he managed to get his leg up that high. Surprise gave way to a momentary loss of control, despite preparing myself for the blow by tightening my abdominal muscles.

He wrapped his meaty hand around the back of my head and pulled me up by my hair. "Enjoy that?"

Pablo had my wrists together and bound by rope. I struggled and the knot tightened. He grabbed my collar and yanked me back, nearly sending me sprawling to the ground. Somehow, I managed to regain my balance.

I assumed a fighter's stance, much to the delight of the men.

Pablo took a few steps back, his smile faded a little with every movement. He came to a stop about six feet away. He lifted his left arm and aimed his gun at my head. Six feet. The perfect distance. A deadly distance. Even if my hands had been untied, he'd still be able to shoot me before I could lay a hand on him.

"This is gonna be fun," Pablo said, the smile returning to his face. "Hector, go help with the car. Get that bitch in back with the kids."

I forgot about Pablo for a minute as my attention shifted to Sarah. She stood with her back against the car, shoulders slumped, head down. She looked like a woman defeated. I didn't like it. It wasn't the look of someone who'd been captured. Everything about her at that moment told me she knew she was about to die.

The heavy guy, Hector, grabbed her by the hair. I guessed that was his thing. With his other hand he pulled the car door open. Immediately the children began screaming, their little voices surfing on top of the salt air and echoing off the high steel and aluminum walls of the warehouses that surrounded us.

Hector forced Sarah into the car. He hit her twice. She went limp. I felt rage rise inside me like bile, bitter and hot and ready to spew out.

"Don't move," Pablo said, without looking at me. The guy must have had faith in his reaction time to take his eyes off me like that.

I didn't move, my feet at least. But my hands went to work dismantling the knot that bound my wrists. Boy scouts these men were not.

Hector slammed the door shut. The voices of the innocent were muffled, for a moment at least. The skinny guy reached into his pocket and pulled out a set of keys. He inserted one into the driver's door and unlocked it. The keys dangled from the lock, reflecting a small, but bright ray of sunlight. He opened the driver's door and slipped inside, leaving one foot on the pavement. His thin arm reached out and around the door frame and he retrieved the keys. It looked like he inserted the one into the ignition, but the car didn't start. A moment later, the guy stepped out of the car and slammed the door shut.

He joined Hector at the back of the vehicle and they started pushing. The car began rolling, slowly at first, toward the edge of the pavement. The men pumped their legs. After twenty feet Hector fell to the ground because the car was moving too fast for him to keep up with. He wallowed on his stomach and then propped himself up using his elbows to watch the car as it headed toward the ocean. The skinny guy let go and straightened up. He placed his hands on his hips and arched his back a little.

The three men watched, stone still, as the car went over the edge of the pavement and into the ocean.

30

THE ROPE THAT HAD BOUND MY WRISTS FELL TO THE ground. None of the men noticed the barely audible sound of it hitting the pavement. Hector and the skinny guy stood on the edge of the road, feet from where Sarah and the kids were encased in a sinking tomb. Tiny hands banged against the rear window, the only sound in an otherwise eerie silence.

Pablo stayed rooted to his spot, six feet away from me. This time the distance wasn't so deadly, not for me at least, because Pablo had his back to me. Maybe he figured it was safe to do so, since my hands had been tied. It was unfair, almost. I thought about giving him a warning, but dismissed that as quickly as he dismissed Sarah and those children.

I passed through the space between us in a second. My torso twisted back to the right, then I whipped around with my left shoulder leading, pulling my right arm around with as much torque as I could muster. Pablo's head whipped to his right, perhaps because he'd heard my foot hit the pavement. My fist connected with his temple. Pablo went down hard, his hip hit, and then his head with a thud. It bounced half a foot in the air and then smacked the pavement again.

I located Pablo's pistol, then located the men. They turned around as if in a daze. They moved in slow motion at first, then picked up their pace. They had close to a hundred feet to cross. It wouldn't take them long, not even Hector with his heft.

I dove toward the gun. The pavement scraped my body and ripped my shirt. I didn't care. Wounds could be cleaned up later. I had to reach the gun before they reached me. My hand wrapped around the pistol and I rolled through the dive. The skinny guy stood closest. I aimed at him first. Time slowed. I saw his long hair bounding and tossing across his face with every step he took. His knees pumped high, arms swung forward then back. I squeezed the trigger and hit him in the chest. The impact of the bullet stopped his torso, but his legs carried through. He flew back and his head crashed into the pavement. Hector grunted as he tried to pick up his pace. I was able to take a second longer to aim and waited until he'd almost reached me. Then I squeezed the trigger. The bullet hit Hector in the forehead. His eyes rolled in and up and his body jerked back, stopped and then fell forward. His knees hit the ground, then his thick chest carried the rest of him forward. A crimson sea formed around his head.

I placed my left hand on the pavement. My right held the gun in front of me, guarding against any sudden movements from the men I'd rendered incapacitated. I had no doubt Hector was dead. His dark, lifeless eyes staring straight ahead told me that. The skinny guy lay on his back. His dull and lifeless eyes fixed on some point beyond the clouds.

I turned my attention to Pablo, who by this time had managed to get to his knees. He faced away from me. I tucked the gun in my waistband and crossed the distance between us in a second or two. I reached down and placed my hands on either side of his head. With a quick and decisive movement, I snapped his neck like a twig.

By now almost half a minute had gone by and no one had drove over to see what was going on. I realized at that moment that this was the plan all along. Get rid of Sarah and the kids, and then shoot me. The men had failed to complete the job, and the rest of them would pay. First, I had to save Sarah and two children trapped in the back of the sinking car.

I sprinted toward the edge of the pavement. The car was underwater, but still visible. I didn't stop when I reached the invisible barrier between land and sea. I dove into the water and swam toward the car. With my pistol, I beat against the rear window until it cracked. I hit it a few more times until there was a decent hole. Water rushed through the opening, flooding the car. The water muffled the screams of tiny voices. I reached into the jagged hole in the window with both hands and began to pull the glass back. A red cloud plumed in the water and floated past my head. I didn't care.

When the hole was wide enough, I reached in and grabbed the little girl and a boy I didn't recognize. The girl squirmed and fought against me. The boy was still, too still. Sarah's body twisted and thrashed. She was trying to get herself in a position to push through the broken window, but her bound hands made it difficult. I had to get the kids to the surface quickly if I was going to have any chance of saving her.

I used my legs against the car to propel us through the water. We flew to the surface. My head burst through and I filled my oxygen-deprived lungs with a gasp, and the girl did too. The boy did nothing. His face was pale. Lips were blue. I looked around, half hoping to see someone at the edge of the pavement. Glad that I didn't, because it would have likely been Reece or Burnett. A rusted ladder was anchored to the concrete piling. I dragged the kids over and pushed the girl halfway to the top. Then I wrapped my left arm through a rung and started performing CPR on the boy.

"C'mon, kid," I yelled between breaths. The little girl, still clinging to the ladder, yelled the same.

A tense moment passed, and then he gagged and coughed and threw up water. His blue eyes fluttered open.

"Can you hang on to the ladder?" I said.

He reached out and grabbed the ladder. His body pulled away an inch or two and then he nodded. "I can do it."

I kicked off the piling and dove into the water. The car had sunk further, no longer buoyant because of the hole I created in the window. It had reached the bottom and settled in on its side. I swam into the rear window. Jagged glass tore through the flesh on my shoulders and my side. I fought against the pain and reached for Sarah's lifeless body. It took a few seconds to free her from the back seat and then get her through the broken window. I wrapped one arm around her chest and swam straight up.

I sucked in air as my head broke through the surface. Sarah's face was a light shade of blue, and her lips were a bit darker. I hoped that I'd freed her in time, but the way she looked gave me doubts.

I pulled her toward the ladder. The kids stood at the top, their timid voices urging me on with words of encouragement. I wrapped my arm through a rung again and used my knees to support Sarah's body. I gave her a few breaths. Nothing happened. I checked for a pulse but couldn't find one. I had to get her on land to begin chest compressions. I placed her over my shoulder and climbed the five feet or so from the ocean to the pavement and placed her body on the ground. Water splashed the pavement and steam rose into the air. I knelt over Sarah's lifeless body. No matter how hard I worked on her, nothing happened. No breath, no pulse, no coughing or choking. The color of her face went from light to dark blue. Her skin felt like ice.

"Cops," the boy said.

"What?" I rose up and looked at him.

"Sirens," he said. "In the distance."

If the cops were on their way, I knew that Burnett would take off whether he was ready or not. No way I'd let him get away with this.

"You," I pointed at the boy. "I need you to keep pushing on her chest like I was doing. OK?"

"OK," he said.

"And you," I pointed at the girl. "You need to give her your breath, like I did. OK?"

"OK," she said.

I got up, grabbed my gun and started running toward Burnett's warehouse. I stopped and turned. "If anyone other than me comes from this way, you run."

31

I HEARD THE MEN FROM THE BOAT TALKING. THEIR VOICES placed them past the edge of a building that sat closer to the water than the others, but still a good distance away from Burnett's warehouse. I pressed back against the steel exterior wall and stepped sideways, moving slowly. I kept my gun up and ready. If I fired, I'd draw the attention of everyone. They had expected the two shots earlier. Those bullets had been meant for me. They wouldn't be receptive to additional gunfire. I wondered why they hadn't moved yet. Wouldn't the other men have returned by now? Perhaps Burnett anticipated a time gap while they disposed of my body. I couldn't go down with the car since the point was for me to watch. They probably had a plan to bring my body to the boat where they'd wrap chains around me and attach them to cinder blocks. I'd sink to the bottom of the Atlantic, lost forever. I found the thought tranquil, in an odd sort of way.

I was close enough to hear what the men were saying. They weren't part of Burnett's inner circle. Instead, they'd been hired to transport him. These weren't good men, not by any stretch of the imagination. They'd done some bad things in the past, and would again in the future, if given the chance. I felt no qualms about killing either one of them. I peeked around the corner. They stood with their backs facing me and at a distance of about four feet. Close enough.

I took a deep breath. The salt air filled my lungs with a slight burn. I looked down and for the first time noticed the gash across my left side. It'd need stitches, but I could manage for now.

I tucked the gun into my waistband and then burst around the corner. My arms whipped around, up and out, the way a master of the butterfly stroke breaks through the water and seemingly flies through the air. My hands wrapped around the outside of their heads, respectively. The momentum carried my hands inward, smashing their heads together. I continued to slide my fingers around, cupped each man under their chin, dragged them around the corner.

I let the guy on the left drop to the ground semi-conscious.

I placed my left hand around the other guy's head. I stood with him in front of me, my arms crisscrossed around his head. He moaned and tried to talk. It came out gurgled. I pulled my arms to the left and right, toward their natural positions. His neck snapped and his body went limp.

I looked down and saw that the other guy had started to crawl away. I took a step, leapt, and came down with my foot on the back of his head. His face crunched against the pavement. Maybe his jaw broke or his orbital socket split in half. Maybe the sound was his teeth snapping off one by one. I didn't look. Didn't care. I reached down and pulled him back by his hair. His body bowed below me, waist on the ground, head pulled back so far it was behind his ass. I gripped his head with both hands and pulled hard to the side. Another snap. Another man who would never take another breath.

I searched their pockets. One had a knife and the other a gun. Perfect. I tucked the knife inside one of my boots. Kept one pistol tucked in my pants and walked with the other in front of me. From this point on, I'd shoot anybody but Burnett on sight.

It took me a couple minutes to reach the warehouse. The area was silent and empty. I stopped in front of the semi and leaned against the chrome grill. Bungee cords dangled. My foot caught one and the metal clasp on the end scraped against the pavement.

I heard a whistle behind me, then the shuffling of feet. "What're you doing, Jack?"

I looked over my shoulder and saw Reece standing there.

"Arms up," he said.

I lifted my arms to the side and said nothing. Hoped like hell he'd play the game.

"Place the gun on the hood of the truck."

I did.

"Now turn around."

I turned.

He smiled. "Burnett's going to love this." He took two steps toward me, then stopped, then leaned to his right, like he was looking past the cab of the over-sized truck. Most important of all, he stopped looking at me.

I pulled my shirt up with my left hand and grabbed the pistol with my right. His head moved first, then his body. His arm followed through last. By that time, I had mine extended. I fired two shots. One caught him in the shoulder; the other missed and slammed into the wall behind him with a thud.

He tried to lift his arm but couldn't. He fired anyway. The bullet smashed into the pavement, sending chips of concrete into the air.

I pulled the trigger again, hitting him in the chest. A red stain bloomed from the center of his shirt. I fired again, this time hitting him in the stomach. He bowed back, but didn't go down. I took one more shot and hit him in the forehead. His head snapped back, and then he collapsed onto his knees and fell forward.

I grabbed the gun off the hood of the truck and walked toward the open warehouse. Burnett stood against the back wall. He clutched the rifle across his chest.

"Don't come in here," he yelled.

"Either shoot me or drop it," I said, taking two steps inside the musty room.

Fear and hatred and rage mixed on his face. I wasn't sure if he was going to take aim or piss himself. He did neither.

"We can work this out, Jack," he said.

"No we can't," I said.

"There's tons of money. I can give it all to you."

"Blood money. The money of how many children's souls, Senator?"

"This has nothing to do with that, Jack."

I stopped and lowered my weapon.

He let the butt of the rifle fall toward the floor, holding it by the barrel with his left hand. He held his other hand out and took a couple steps forward, slightly bent at the waist, trying not to look intimidating, I supposed.

"Listen, Jack, there's no reason that you and I-"

"Why'd you do it?" I said.

He paused and tilted his head. "Money."

"What was your plan?"

He nodded and looked over my shoulder. "My boy's on the boat. We planned to sail down south. Hole up for a while and at the same time, a radical group was going to claim they'd kidnapped us. No ransom or any bullshit like that."

"This group," I said, "these are the men you sold the kids to?"

He nodded. "One of them, at least."

"OK. Then what?"

He took a few more steps forward. Stopped and swallowed. "After a few months I'd return home. I'd have to get beaten up a bit, but in the end I'd free me and my boy and make it out alive."

"Why drag your son into it?"

"It's the only way."

"Only way for what?"

He took another step, but this time I held out my pistol to stop him. His hand went up and he took a step back.

"The only way for us to reunite, you see," he said.

"No, I don't see. What do you mean reunite? You and Christopher?"

"Yeah."

This time, I took a step back. "What about the garbage you fed me earlier about how you'd adopt him?"

He smiled and dipped his head an inch. "See, as far as anyone will know, I didn't take him, Jack. Someone kidnapped him, and I risked my life to rescue him. In the process, I was taken as well. But those bastards slipped up and I killed them and got us out alive."

"And you come home a hero," I said. "And everyone will brush off the fact that you'd had an affair with a woman ten years ago and fathered a child with her. And while you'd been abducted, someone came along and killed her."

"Great minds and all that."

I heard the slight sound of shuffling behind me. Burnett smiled and looked over my shoulder. It wasn't much, a second, but it told me plenty.

I dropped to one knee and spun. Saw a man I'd never seen before. He held a gun and aimed it at me. I fired before he did. The bullet hit him in the chest and he fell backward upon impact. I spun again and saw Burnett holding the rifle with both hands, taking aim. I squeezed the trigger and hit him in the right shoulder. He dropped the rifle and staggered backward until he reached the wall.

"You son of a bitch," he yelled.

I crossed the room. He kept sliding along the wall until he found the corner. I grabbed him by his collar and threw him to the ground. Ran up and kicked him from behind.

"Move!" I said.

He scrambled to his knees. Blood poured from his wound, staining his shirt and coating his arm in crimson. There was cursing mixed with yells of pain. We reached the open doorway. I kicked him from behind again, sending him headfirst into the pavement. I walked up behind him and grabbed his collar a second time. Pulled him to his feet and pushed him toward the semi.

"Walk," I said.

"Where're we going?" he said.

"To the truck."

"Jack," he said. "I'll give you anything. Anything you want."

We were next to the cab of the truck. I reached out, grabbed his left shoulder and spun him around.

"Anything?" I said.

"Name it. I'm good for it, Jack."

"Bring Sarah back to life."

"I... I..."

"Yeah. That's what I thought."

I shoved him against the side of the truck's cab. His right shoulder slammed into it and he yelled in pain. I grabbed him by his hair again and dragged him to the front of the truck. Blood from the bullet hole in his shoulder smeared along the white fiberglass. I pushed him back against the chrome grill, then threw an uppercut into his chin. His body slumped to the ground.

There were six bungee cords attached to the truck's grill. They were various lengths and colors and designs. I hooked them all to one side in a straight up and down line, letting one end of each dangle.

Burnett lay on the ground, groaning. I reached down, pulled him up, and hoisted him a foot off the ground. I held him there with one hand, while I strapped the first cord across his shoulder. I looped the cord through the grill a few times to tighten it, then attached it on the other side. I pulled his left arm out and secured it. Then I stretched another cord over his waist, then his thighs and calves. Finally, I secured his right hand.

I took a few steps back and smiled at my handiwork. He was fixed to the grill of the truck, arms out, legs tight together, and his feet off the ground.

"What the hell are you doing, Jack?" he said for the twentieth time.

This time I answered him. "One thing your research didn't tell you about me, Senator. I kill in kind."

"What?"

I ignored him, stepped around the side of the truck, pulled myself up into the cab. Once behind the wheel, I fired the big diesel engine up, and it roared to life like a pride of lions rising for the hunt. I looked around, but didn't see what I needed inside the truck, so I scanned the area around the buildings. Saw a cinder block and knew that would work for my purposes. I got out and ran over to the block. Burnett watched me the entire way back. This time he said nothing.

I hopped back into the cab and put the truck in first gear. It jerked into motion and I steered it in a half circle, then straightened it out so that we were driving away from the kids and Sarah's body. I got the truck to a steady speed and opened the door. I stood in the open doorway, one hand on the wheel, the other on the cinder block. I dropped the block on the gas and hopped onto the concrete. My body slammed into the ground hard. I was sure I had a few new scrapes and possibly a broken bone. The sound of Burnett's screams rising above that old diesel engine made it worth it, though. I rolled too far and almost went over the edge into the water. I scrambled to my feet and followed the truck with my eyes.

Its path was taking it closer and closer to the edge, but there was another building that stood out further than the others did. At this point, it was a tossup whether it would hit the building or plunge into the ocean. I watched with heightened anticipation. The truck had veered far enough over that if it hit the building, Burnett wouldn't be smashed into the steel exterior. Finally, the truck passed by and inched closer to the edge of the road. Twenty seconds later, the first tire went over the edge, and then the next. Finally, the big truck teetered on the edge, scraping the pavement and sending sparks into the air. And then it went over. The grill went in first and dove toward the bottom.

I turned and headed toward the kids and Sarah's body. I stopped at the boat and called for Christopher. The boy came above deck. I told him everything was all right. I helped him off the boat and carried him down the stretch of pavement between the warehouses and the ocean.

We reached the kids and Sarah's body as the cops did. All eyes fell on me, and their guns followed.

I set the kid down, then held up my hands. "My name's Jack Noble," I said. "I'm a federal agent. They took my wallet, but if you call Frank Skinner, he'll provide all the information you need." I gave them the number to reach Frank.

They told me to stay put, but I didn't. The boy pointed toward Sarah's body, which still lay on the pavement. Her skin was pale and her lips were no longer blue. Her chest rose and fell in an awkward cadence. She was alive.

32

By four p.m. that afternoon, Frank had a private jet waiting for us at an executive airport north of the city. He got the cops off my back and somehow managed to get them to escort us, first to the hospital and then to the airport once Sarah had been cleared.

I had been concerned that she wouldn't be able to return to us. She was still unconscious when they loaded her into the ambulance, and there was the possibility that she'd suffered some brain damage. The kids had kept working on her after I left to take care of Burnett. They didn't give up on her and she came through.

Doc had to pull a few strings to get Sarah out of the hospital, including agreeing to have a traveling nurse accompany us. She was young and pretty and nice to Sarah and the kids. I told her I didn't need any attention. She looked me up and down with a quizzical eye, but agreed to leave me alone.

I fell asleep in less than five minutes after takeoff and didn't wake up until we touched down outside of D.C.

Frank was the first to greet me when I stepped off the plane.

"We're going to blow the doors off this," he said.

I nodded, scanning the lot to see if there were any waiting parents.

"Working on a warrant for Burnett's office and his house and his car and anything else we can get our hands on."

"He's dead," I said.

Frank nodded. "C'mon, Jack, we'll discuss that later."

"What about the kids? Where're their parents?"

"We're taking them back to headquarters first."

Two black SUVs waited at the edge of the runway. The kids rode in one, me, Frank, and Sarah in the other. The nurse tagged along with us.

"Can you take me home?" Sarah asked.

"No," Frank said. "We're dropping the nurse at Dulles, then taking you back to our office. You go home when Doc clears you."

And what he didn't say was when we cleared her, she had to be debriefed and she had to sign a ton of forms that essentially made it illegal for her to talk about anything that had happened since she'd met us.

It took two-and-a-half hours to reach the office. Traffic was a bitch. But it gave us time to get a couple FBI special agents to our office.

Special Agents Duncan and Bishop met us in the lobby. I'd worked with Duncan on a few occasions. He'd been around the block a few times, to say the least. When he saw the kids come through the door, he smiled.

"Almost thirty years in," he said. "Never get tired of a happy ending."

Bishop was new and young and looked to be fresh out of law school. He smiled nervously and asked where he should take the kids to begin the process of reuniting them with their parents.

Frank led them to an interrogation room.

"The boy stays with us," I said.

Duncan frowned. "You know that's not how this works, Noble."

"We know his mother. It'd be better if we did this in person. You can come with us. In fact, I'd like you to be there. A cop, too."

He cocked his head and so did Frank.

"What's going on, Jack?" Frank said.

"Why don't we go now?" I said.

The men agreed. Duncan checked with Bishop and made sure his younger partner could handle the kids by himself.

Traffic had thinned, and it took less than half an hour to reach Tammy Nockowitz's townhouse. Frank pulled into the driveway. We waited two more minutes for a local cop to arrive. We met the cop at the bottom of the driveway and I asked him to watch the boy for a few minutes while we spoke with the mother.

Frank knocked on the door and took a step back. Tammy pulled the door open, looked at the three of us standing there and then looked like she was going to cry.

"What's happened?" she said.

"Tammy," I said. "Christopher's OK."

She fell to her knees and cried.

"His father's dead," I said.

She rocked back on her heels and looked up at us. She bit her bottom lip. Mascara stained her face. She wiped her cheeks with her palms and then brushed strands of loose hair behind her ears.

"How?" she said.

"Some of that's classified," Frank said. "And until it passes through the proper channels, we can't discuss it."

She lifted herself off the floor. "Where's my son? When can I see him?"

"In a minute," Frank said. "Jack, you want to get this going?"

I cleared my throat stepped forward so I was right in front of her. I wanted to look into her eyes. I had to see the look on her face.

"Why'd you agree to it, Tammy?"

A confused look crossed her face and she shook her head. "What?"

"This is your chance," I said. "Tell us now and we'll see what we can do for you."

"I don't know what you're talking about, Mr. Noble."

I took a step back, feigning shock. "How do you know my name?" I looked at Frank. "Our names were never given out, were they?"

"No," Frank said with a confused look.

"Tammy?" I said.

Frank placed his hand on my shoulder and leaned in toward me. "What are you getting at?"

"Tammy and Burnett never stopped seeing each other. Isn't that right, Tammy?"

It didn't occur to me until we'd reached the plane that Tammy had been involved with this from day one. She thought Burnett was coming back for her, but in reality, he was trying to have her killed once he realized she'd told us too much.

She shook her head. "No, you got that wrong. Yeah, we had an affair, but that was ten years ago, a one-time thing. I got pregnant and told him, and he wanted nothing to do with me and Christopher."

The look was there. Deception. Burnett wasn't talking about reuniting with Christopher. They'd never been together, thus nullifying the opportunity at a reunion. He meant Tammy. And still, he didn't really mean a reunion. The fact was that they'd never stopped seeing each other. Sure, he wasn't involved in

Christopher's life, but the affair he'd had with the boy's mother had stretched on for a decade.

"No, he didn't want the public to find out about you and Christopher, but he still wanted something to do with you. See, being married while having a child with another woman would have been political suicide for Burnett. Continuing to see that woman while remaining married, well he could kiss away any chance he had of being anything other than a mayor in a town with a population of three people. And he wasn't willing to risk that until now."

"No, no, no," she said. "You got it all wrong."

"Why'd you do it?" I said.

She shook her head. "I didn't do anything."

My voice escalated to a scream. "Why'd you let him take your son?"

"I didn't."

"You staged it so that Pablo hit you on the head. Hell, you even got a little cut out of it, didn't you? Pablo didn't work for the guys in the house. He worked for Burnett. I saw him down in Miami." I stopped and stared at her. When she didn't speak, I continued. "You let Burnett take your son, and then after we'd rescued him, you let him take him again."

"No," she said. "I didn't let him take him again. That's why he had me run off the road. I said I wouldn't do it again."

"Again," I repeated. "You left the dinner with Christopher, but when the paramedics arrived, he wasn't in the car. They even said if he had been, he'd have died."

She covered her face with her hands and sobbed heavily.

"Duncan," Frank said. "Why don't you take her to the car for us?"

Duncan entered the house and eased Tammy's hands to her side and then in front of her. He placed handcuffs around her wrists and guided her by her elbow.

She stopped and looked over her shoulder at me.

"I wanted to be a family, Jack. He said Christopher would be OK the first time. They'd treat him well."

"They didn't," I said. "I found him in a dirt pit dug out in a basement."

"And I didn't want this to happen again," she said. "That's why I was trying to talk to you at the dinner. You could have prevented all this."

I shook my head, said nothing. I was done with her. The FBI could take it from there.

Frank told Duncan to wait while he spoke with the police officer. The officer agreed to take Christopher and me back to SIS headquarters, while Frank and Duncan escorted Tammy Nockowitz to jail.

33

THEY GAVE ME A WEEK OFF TO REST MY BODY AND CLEAR MY head. I spent most of the first day in bed, sleeping for close to sixteen hours, then getting up and going back to bed after only four alcohol-fueled hours. I don't remember what I dreamed about, but I woke up every few hours that night, soaked in sweat, with the overwhelming feeling I'd been drowning. The thought that I'd started suffering from post-traumatic stress disorder crossed my mind, but I brushed it aside. I'd seen and been through far worse than the events of the past week.

The next day I took a drive into northern Virginia and stopped at Sarah's firehouse. The guys there told me that she was off for a couple weeks. I convinced one of them to give me her home address.

I drove to her apartment building and parked in front of the main entrance to the building her unit was located in. I took my time walking up the three flights of stairs that led to her door. I thought about what to say to her. Twenty or so opening lines went from winners to losers in the span of two minutes. In the end, I settled on *hi*. I figured she'd understand.

I knocked on the door. A minute passed with no answer. I hadn't bothered watching the peephole, so I wasn't sure if no one was home, or someone looked through, saw me standing there, and decided not to answer. After another round of knocking, a woman I didn't recognize opened the door.

"Sarah here?"

She shook her head.

"Know when she'll be back?"

"She left yesterday. Said she was going home to see her parents."

"Where's that?"

The woman looked at me like I was crazy and started to close the door.

"Wait," I said.

She stopped and arched her eyebrows with a slight shake of her head.

"Can you tell her Jack came by?"

"Oh," she said. "You're Jack Noble?"

I nodded.

"Wait here."

I waited.

She returned with an envelope. "This is for you."

As soon as I grabbed the cream-colored envelope, she slammed the door shut. I waited outside the apartment for a few minutes, listening for voices inside. I didn't hear any and decided to leave.

I sat in my car for five minutes, staring at the envelope that had my name written across the front. I opened it and pulled out a single folded piece of notebook paper. I carefully read the words Sarah had written for me.

Jack,

I've never met a man who excited me the way you did. When I was around you, I felt that I could do anything. Accomplish anything. Be anything. At first, I felt like I was in an action movie. You were the hero, and I was the woman who got mixed up in your dangerous world.

But, like all smart heroines, I came to my senses. I can't be with a man like you. The job you have, and the risks you take, it's all too much for me. No matter how hard I try, I can't envision a future with you as a part of my life.

Please don't try to find me, Jack. Don't search for my parents. Don't return to my apartment. Don't go back to the firehouse. I think it's best if you simply forgot about me.

-S

I half expected it, in a way. Sarah had gone through a lot, and it was my fault. I believed that even if we had started seeing each other, she'd have held some resentment toward me for what happened to her in Miami. Part of me had wanted to make these same points to her, but in the end, my desire for her had won out. And now I'd never know if there could have been a future for us together.

I opened the car door and swung my legs over and set them down on the pavement. I pulled a lighter out of my pocket and ignited it. The flame hovered below the letter for a moment, then the paper burst into flames. I held it in front of me until the fire grazed the tips of my fingers and I let the ball of flames fall to the ground and watched it until it was nothing more than black ash. I stomped it out for good measure, then said, "Goodbye, Sarah."

Alcohol got me through the night. I managed seven hours of uninterrupted sleep. The next day I drove to SIS headquarters. Frank came out of his office when he saw me step into the lobby.

"Jack?" he said. "What the hell are you doing here? You're supposed to be off."

"Got bored," I said.

"Come on, let's sit in my office for a few."

I followed him into his office. He closed the door and then walked around the desk where he took a seat across from me.

"Burnett wasn't just involved in this thing," he said.

"Oh yeah?"

"Son of a bitch masterminded it. We got everything. Records of every shipment. Names of the kids. Names of suppliers and purchasers. I got back from setting up the biggest damn operation you ever heard of. FBI and local law enforcement all across the U.S. The CIA is helping globally. We even got Special Forces joining in, from all branches. We're bringing them home, Jack. All of the kids are coming home."

"That's a lot of happy phone calls," I said.

Frank leaned forward. He narrowed his eyes and said, "What's going on? I thought you'd be excited."

"I am," I said.

"Then what is it?"

"I can't get past the fact that Sarah almost died, and it was all my fault."

Frank shook his head. "You can't blame yourself. Plus, she made it through OK. Some would argue that if you hadn't been there, she'd have died."

"She wouldn't have been there if it weren't for me."

Frank shrugged.

"She won't talk to me."

He nodded. "Sometimes that happens."

I nodded back.

"Hey," Frank said. "Why don't you head this operation up? You did so much to bring it down, it only makes sense that-"

"I'm done, Frank."

His body straightened, like he'd been taken a knife to the lower back. "What?"

I pulled my ID and badge out and placed them on his desk.

His eyes followed my outstretched arms and settled on the items I'd put in front of him. I pulled my pistol from its holster and sat it next to my ID.

"Jack," he said. "Why don't you think this over for a while? You don't have to take over the operation. Take a vacation instead. Hell, you've been with me for over two years and these last few days are the only time you've had off."

I shook my head. "I'm done." I grabbed the arms of the chair and pushed myself up, then pulled the door open and stepped into the lobby. I crossed the room and stopped halfway. Turned and looked back, first at my office, empty and dark, and then at Frank, who stood in his open doorway. The expression on his face was one of pain and confusion. I'd seen that look several times, usually when I left somewhere or someone. In this case, I was doing both.

I walked through the short hallway and stopped in front of the door that led to the garage. The overhead fan kicked on, a fierce *whirr* that settled into a hum after a few seconds. I grabbed the door handle and started to turn it.

"Wait," Frank called after me.

"What?" I said without turning around.

"The President wants to meet us next week."

"No thanks." I pulled the door open and stepped into the garage. The door slammed shut behind me. I figured it'd open again before I reached my car. It didn't.

I spent a few hours on the beltway, driving around D.C. while the traffic was light, searching for a moment of clarity. I didn't manage to find one.

Later that night I sat alone in my apartment, drinking. Frank called a few times. I answered once and told him not to come over. Then the phone rang again after I told him to leave me alone. I answered, ready to yell at him for harassing me.

"It's Bear."

I said nothing.

"What the hell happened, man? Guys are saying something big went down with a Senator and that you were at the heart of it. What's the deal?"

"I don't think I'm allowed to say, at least, not yet. Definitely not over the phone."

"You OK?"

"I'll be fine."

"OK," he said. "Just wanted to check up on you."

I said nothing.

"I guess I'll give you a call in a week or two?"

"I quit my job," I said.

Bear said nothing.

"You still interested in going into business together?"

"Yeah," he said.

"How much longer until you're out?"

"I got three months, then I'm a free man. No more Marines. No more CIA."

"Meet me in Key West."

"When?"

"When you're no longer the government's overgrown step-child."

He chuckled. "Where'll I find you?"

"I'll be sitting outside a bar."

THE END

Jack Noble's story continues in *Thin Line* (*Jack Noble #3*) - excerpt and link below!

Want to be among the first to download the next Jack Noble book? Sign up for L.T. Ryan's newsletter, and you'll be notified the minute new releases are available - and often at a discount for the first 48 hours! As a thank you for signing up, you'll receive a complimentary copy of *The Recruit: A Jack Noble Short Story*.

Join here: http://ltryan.com/newsletter/

I enjoy hearing from readers. Feel free to drop me a line at ltryan70@gmail.com. I read and respond to every message.

If you enjoyed reading *A Deadly Distance*, I would appreciate it if you would help others enjoy these books, too. How?

Lend it. This e-book is lending-enabled, so please, feel free to share it with a friend. All they need is an amazon account and a Kindle, or Kindle reading app on their smart phone or computer.

Recommend it. Please help other readers find this book by recommending it to friends, readers' groups and discussion boards.

Review it. Please tell other readers why you liked this book by reviewing it at Amazon, Barnes & Noble, Apple or Goodreads. Your opinion goes a long way in helping others decide if a book is for them. Also, a review doesn't have to be a big old book report. If you do write a review, please send me an email at ltryan70@gmail.com so I can thank you with a personal email.

Like Jack. Visit the Jack Noble Facebook page and give it a like: https://www.facebook.com/JackNobleBooks.

ALSO BY L.T. RYAN

The Jack Noble Series

The Recruit (free)

The First Deception (Prequel 1)

Noble Beginnings

A Deadly Distance

Ripple Effect (Bear Logan)

Thin Line

Noble Intentions

When Dead in Greece

Noble Retribution

Noble Betrayal

Never Go Home

Beyond Betrayal (Clarissa Abbot)

Noble Judgment

Never Cry Mercy

Deadline

End Game

Mitch Tanner Series

The Depth of Darkness

Into The Darkness

Deliver Us From Darkness - coming soon

Affliction Z Series

THIN LINE: CHAPTER 1

December 31, 2006

"The target's name is Brett Taylor, and this'll be your toughest assignment yet."

Frank Skinner set the blue folder in front of me, opened to Taylor's service record. A paper clip held a small photo to the upper left side of the folder. A head shot of a face chiseled from stone, with eyes that gave a glimpse into a heart made of ice. I read over the file, then glanced at the picture again. I might as well have been looking into a mirror. There were a few similarities between me and the target. Physically we were identical: 6'2", 220. We'd both enlisted in the military at the age of eighteen. He went into the Army; I became a Marine. We had both been selected for special assignment during boot camp.

I turned to the next page. It was blank. Every single one that followed was as well. There were only a few reasons for that.

"I'm not kidding, Jack," Frank continued. He pushed off the desktop and rolled backward. A rusted wheel squeaked until his chair collided into the wall with a soft thud. "This guy makes you look like a teddy bear. While you were off playing with the CIA guarding doors in Baghdad and whatnot, Taylor was doing black ops so insidious that any record indicating they'd ever even been thought of has been incinerated. When you were playing anti-terrorist agent along with me, he was taking down cell leaders before they even knew that they wanted to blow something up. He's the ultimate government weapon. And my understanding is that lately those hostile to the Nation's interests were not his only targets."

I looked up from the documents and met Frank's stare. His dark eyes didn't waver. I saw fear, perhaps. Anytime we had one of these meetings, Frank looked serious. Lips, nose, jaw, eyebrows, all could be manipulated. But his tone and gestures conveyed more concern than I'd ever seen from him. And we had a history that went back nearly five years to the summer of 2002, when he had hand-selected me to join him as his partner in the SIS. Together, we'd faced our share of men who had no regard for the welfare of others - so many that Frank's warning list read like the back of a cereal box.

What was so different about Brett Taylor?

"Can you give any examples?"

Frank leaned back in his chair and placed both hands behind his shaking head. "You know I can't do that."

"A hint, then?"

Frank said nothing. He bit at his bottom lip - a tell that he was considering revealing more than he should. I had to press.

"Hell, give me a country, Frank. I can take it from there."

For guys like us, news headlines read like a *Who's Doing What* in the espionage and assassin community. Nothing was ever as tidy as they made it sound in the papers and on TV.

Frank shook his head. "Can't do it. Not yet, at least. You live to finish the job, then we'll talk."

I closed the folder, pushed it toward Frank. "Nothing but a bunch of blank pages in there."

"That's to make a point."

"Which is?"

"Don't underestimate this guy. Every single one of those blank pages, and there's at least fifty, could be filled with details of the assignments this guy has completed."

"I get it. He's a badass. Jesus, Frank. How long have I been doing this?" I rose and shoved the chair to the side with my leg, and then leaned back against the glass wall and shoved my hands in my pockets. The glass felt cold against the back of my arms.

Frank remained silent. Thick jaw muscles rippled at the corners of his face as he stared me down. There was plenty about Taylor, and the job, that he wasn't willing to share. Or had been prohibited from revealing. At times, things worked that way. We'd all become accustomed to it. And it was beneficial. The less I knew about a target, the easier it was to complete the assignment. The less Frank knew, the less guilt there might be over handing it over to me. I operated with the general understanding that if a government agency signed off on an order and sent me to someone's door, there was a pretty good reason. The justice I was dispatched to enforce was quick and generally merciful.

We should all be so lucky.

So, Brett Taylor, while he provided service to his country for over a decade, must've done something pretty heinous for me to be sitting across from Frank, staring at a blank service record.

I sat down, placed my arm on the desk, leaned forward. "Where and when?"

"New York," he said. "Brooklyn. Close to Prospect Park. He's due back ten days from now, on Tuesday, the ninth."

I had a place in New York. A few friends there, too. It'd be better if they didn't know I was coming into town, though. Not for something like this.

"Know his itinerary?" I said.

"Not yet, but we'll get it."

"He in the States now?"

"Coming in international."

"From where?"

"Not sure yet."

"I'll have Bear tail him."

Frank pressed his lips together so tightly they turned white. He'd never been a fan of my partner, Riley "Bear" Logan, whose nickname suited the guy in more ways than one. The big man and I had been best friends since boot camp. After I left the SIS, we went into business for ourselves. I trusted him with my life, and I didn't care what any of my contacts thought. Bear handled himself and got results. We were a great team.

Better than Frank and I ever were.

"He's in," I said. "Or I'm out."

Frank took a few deep, ragged breaths, and then nodded. "I'll make sure you have the flight info in time. I'm waiting on additional details of Taylor's offices, residences, and so on, in case there are alternatives. I'll fax them over as soon as I get them. Meanwhile, limit how many sources you reach out to. As you can imagine, if something this high-profile leaks, we'll all go down for it."

"Got it." I rose, turned, grabbed the door handle and pulled it open an inch. The air from the overhead vent shot past me on the path of least resistance.

Take one more shot at it, I thought.

Letting the door fall closed, I turned around. "What'd this guy do?"

Frank diverted his focus to his computer monitor and shook his head.

"Come on, Frank. Just between you and me."

A single laugh escaped past his pursed lips. He shuffled his mouse around on a gray square pad, clicking the left and right buttons. "You know people end up on these lists at times because of conversations that go too far. If I say anything more, it'll be someone like Brett Taylor paying a visit to both of us."

"Fair enough." I turned my back to him.

"Jack."

I didn't look back. "Yeah?"

"Close this one out, and maybe I'll tell you everything over a pitcher or three. In the meantime, happy New Year."

THIN LINE: CHAPTER 2

Located on 4th Street between 6th and 7th Avenue, the five-story brownstone loomed like weathered ruins amid the surrounding rehabbed and renovated buildings. The owner had received multiple unsolicited offers to purchase for reasonable sums, but he had refused to sell. The building held too much value for him. Presumably Brett Taylor didn't care that the building was in shambles, or that nine of the ten apartments inside matched the rough exterior. I guess everything he needed existed in that tenth pristine apartment.

Between Frank and one of my sources, I had a five-year history on the building as well as the day-to-day nuances of life within its walls.

When the block showed no human activity, I crossed the street and forced my way inside the brownstone. A combination of human waste, sweat, mildew, and cigarette smoke pelted me, and I nearly gagged at the overwhelming stench. After a few moments I adjusted, and then continued past the entrance hall, which branched in two, one passage leading east and the other west.

The first floor had four apartments. From the looks of things, transients and homeless occupied these units when Taylor wasn't there. Same with the two units on the second floor. The fourth and fifth floors contained a single residence each. For whatever reason, Taylor had chosen to forgo the supposed prestige of a penthouse, and lived in an apartment on the third floor.

I started my search in the west hall. My primary concern was security equipment - anything that would give our position away or record our actions when Bear and I returned to complete the job. I saw no cameras on the outside, and none at the entrance. Presumably, Taylor had some sort of a monitoring system in place. Men in his position had to.

The apartments on the first floor had all been occupied recently, although they were empty at the moment. Leftover cellophane wrappers, soda cans, and liquor bottles were strewn about. Body odor lingered, a stench nearly as foul as that at the main entrance.

At the end of the east hall was a door that opened up to stairs leading to the basement. I followed them down, sticking to the edges to minimize squeaking. The room below the building was wide open from foundation wall to foundation wall, aside from evenly spaced support columns that resembled an old man's bowed legs. An old furnace sat dormant in the middle of the rear wall, the bricks surrounding it several shades darker than the rest. The floor was covered in an inch of soot and dust. Pristine. No footprints. Clearly no one ventured into the brownstone's basement these days. I walked along the perimeter of the room and remained on the lookout for electrical wires and communication lines. Only thing I found was brick and mortar and dust.

Satisfied that the basement was just that, I hiked back up the stairs, bypassing the first floor landing, and made my way through the building's second level.

Again, I found the rooms looking recently occupied, but currently empty. Perhaps Taylor had a system of letting the homeless that frequented his building know when he'd return. *Use my place, but don't dare be there when I get back.* Perhaps his way of repenting for the sins he committed for our government.

I made the journey from the second floor to the third with more trepidation. So far, there were no signs of security. That had to change. Still, I didn't find anything.

Of the two units on the third floor, one was used by Taylor.

I searched the unoccupied third floor apartment first. Unlike the units of the first two levels, no one had been inside this space for quite some time. Maybe not since the last tenant, who might even have died in the room. Cobwebs hung from the ceiling and draped the walls. Roaches scattered as light penetrated the space for the first time in perhaps years. I couldn't see them, but their thin legs scratched the hardwood floor with a sound like someone clawing their way out of a wooden box.

The place was fully furnished. The furnishings had to be sixty or seventy years old, with a few turn-of-the-century pieces. The kind of stuff my mother had, but never let me or my brother or my sister sit on. *And don't let your friends near it, Jack!* Antique picture frames housed yellowing photographs. A young woman. A young man. A young couple, together. Her in her wedding dress, him in his suit. Her perched on his lap. A baby. A child. A teenager. The sequence was repeated at the other end in reverse. One boy, one girl. One happy couple aging decades in a series of photographs perched on the mantle. A casket cross etched with the name "Robert." He died first. She remained in the apartment, loyal to him, waiting to return to him, until her final day passed.

I returned to the hallway. Examined the area surrounding

the front door of Taylor's apartment. Again, I found nothing. He'd concealed his security and monitoring devices well. When Bear and I returned, we'd have to bring equipment to aid in our search, and disrupt any communications equipment he had on site.

The search concluded with a quick tour of the fourth and fifth floors. These were big hollow spaces void of furnishings. After passing through the fourth floor, I expected the top level to be full of computers or weapons or an army, even. None of that. And no signs anyone had been up there in some time. A fine layer of dust coated the hardwood floors, and cobwebs lined the walls, though not to the extent of the third floor apartment. Perhaps my intel was wrong. Maybe these spaces were used regularly. That, or someone must regularly be cleaning the space on the upper levels.

The narrow hallway on the top floor had roof access. An old rusted ladder mounted to the rear wall. I climbed it and popped the hatch to the roof. Strong gusts of wind passed by. A steady stream pelted down on me. The cold wormed its way into my clothing. I performed a quick recon of the roof's perimeter and determined there was no way off unless one was willing to risk a drop of seventy feet or so to the concrete below by attempting a ten-foot jump to the next building.

I double-checked every the room on the way down. All except Taylor's. I wasn't looking for signs of life. Instead, I wanted to root out any possible escape routes. Iron bars on the upper level windows made any attempt from there impossible. The fire escapes on the second and third floors had been removed. Heavy bolts stuck out of the wall as a reminder they had once been attached. An alley around the length and width of the Brownstone, but there was no outlet. It formed a U that originated and terminated on 4th Street.

So that left one way in and out of the building: the front

door. And once we saw Brett Taylor enter through it, that spelled game over.

~

Click here to purchase Thin Line now!

Visit http://ltryan.com/noble-intentions/ for purchasing information for the Jack Noble series.

ABOUT THE AUTHOR

L.T. Ryan is a *USA Today* and international bestselling author. The new age of publishing offered L.T. the opportunity to blend his passions for creating, marketing, and technology to reach audiences with his popular Jack Noble series.

Living in central Virginia with his wife, the youngest of his three daughters, and their three dogs, L.T. enjoys staring out his window at the trees and mountains while he should be writing, as well as reading, hiking, running, and playing with gadgets. See what he's up to at http://ltryan.com.

Social Medial Links:

- Facebook (L.T. Ryan): https://www.facebook.com/LTRyanAuthor
- Facebook (Jack Noble Page): https://www.facebook.com/JackNobleBooks/
- Twitter: https://twitter.com/LTRyanWrites
- Goodreads: http://www.goodreads.com/author/show/6151659.L_T_Ryan